27-

THE DRUNKEN SPELUNKER'S GUIDE TO PLATO

a novel

KATHY GIUFFRE

THE CAVE

THIS WAS IN THE DAYS WHEN NIGHTTIME used to mean something. At midnight, the television stations all played "The Star-Spangled Banner" and then went dark until time for the Farmers' Weather Report at dawn. You couldn't go to the grocery store after nine. All the other stores closed at eight. It might be hard to find an open gas station. Last call was taken seriously at all the local bars—people were known to get busted running red lights, trying to make it in time.

In Waterville, the only all-night restaurant of any kind was Clyde's Chicken, a brightly lit fried-chicken joint that usually had only one thing on the menu—Chicken and Biscuits. Sometimes a handwritten sign taped up on the wall announced the temporary addition of Fried Livers and Gizzards. I never saw anyone eat them, although I have heard some, such as Stinky, claim to. He felt it gave him an air of distinction.

Some men woo women with wine or with roses or with dates to see movies in which the heroine, despite being movie-star beautiful, is saved from a loveless future only by falling into the last-chance arms of the sweet and quirky hero, who is inexplicably available despite also being movie-star beautiful.

These men show a lack of imagination.

Danny wooed me with a handful of early-spring violets and a 2 A.M. trip to Clyde's Chicken.

"Are you going to eat the gizzards to impress me?" I asked.

"Lord, no," he said, and shuddered.

The Cavern Tavern was underground. You entered the front (where the bar was) down a dingy flight of concrete stairs from the street above, breathing in an updraft of cigarette smoke, dampness, stale beer fumes, and subterranean cool. You entered the back (where the pool tables were) down a set of wooden steps jutting out of the wet alleyway asphalt next to the dumpsters. Over the back door was a sign that read, "Ballroom Entrance."

The Cave should have been a sad place in the late afternoons when Rafi, the weary first-shift bartender, opened both doors to try to let some air in while he washed out last night's dirty ashtrays in the tiny cold-water sink next to the toilets. It should have been happy—happiest—at night when the red-colored light bulbs strung across the ceiling were turned on and the place was packed tight with tipsy, laughing people who had come to hear the bands play. We passed the hat and, on a good night, the band made sixty dollars altogether, plus the right to stay around after closing and drink free beer.

But in the afternoons, before opening time, if Rafi liked you, you could sit at the bar and smoke cigarettes and read the newspaper or listen to the call-in shows on the radio or to the preachers who made me laugh out loud and made Rafi grin and shake his head in disbelief, which was the closest he ever got to laughing out loud himself. Sometimes, if you felt like it, you could help Rafi out by taking the green plastic covers off the pool tables and folding them and brushing the tables down with the pool-table brush and then, while Rafi had their coin boxes open and was busy raking out all the quarters and counting them and putting them into rolls to take to the bank, you could play a free game of pool. In the summer especially, it would stay light so long that sometimes the afternoon didn't end until late at night.

I used to hang around with Rafi when I first came to Waterville, and I was on hand when the regular weeknight bartender, Roscoe, quit unexpectedly after passing the bar exam. It was his fourth stab at it, so everyone was caught off guard. The next we heard of him, he had been elected to Congress and moved to Washington.

The afternoon when Roscoe came in with the happy news, I was there.

"How about hiring Josie?" Rafi said.

I took the job because I didn't have another one.

Danny said, "Why don't you skip work and just stay home in bed with me?"

" 'Cause I'll get fired and I need the money, that's why," I said.

"What can money buy you that would be better than a long afternoon with just you and me together right here in this room?"

"Well, just for instance, maybe it could pay the rent to stay underneath this roof."

"It's mighty romantic to sleep under the stars," Danny grinned.

"What about when it rains?"

"You just have an answer for everything, don't you, sugar?"

"Maybe I do."

"Well, that's a relief. A smart woman like you can surely figure out a way to keep the rain off us."

Then he rolled over and went back to sleep.

Imagine, Socrates begins, a race of human beings who have lived all their lives deep inside a cave, chained so they cannot move their arms or legs or even turn their heads, but are compelled to stare straight ahead at a blank stone wall in front of them. Imagine also that behind these prisoners blazes a bonfire. Between the place where the bonfire roars and the place where the people sit, there is a walkway across which other people walk carrying all manner of objects, statues, and figures of stone and wood, casting long shadows on to the wall in front of the prisoners.

Socrates imagines that the chained prisoners in the cave talk with each other, discussing the shadows they see on the wall in front of them. The shadows would seem to be real to the chained observers, Socrates argues. And the sounds made by the bearers of the objects, echoing off the walls of the cave, would be taken to be the voices of the shadows. The prisoners believe these shadows and echoes to be reality.

They can't see each other in the gloom, but even in their chains, they feel one another's presence and seek out the sounds of each other's voices. They converse on all manner of topics, he says, suggested to them by the shadows of themselves and of the objects behind them and by the echoes of the voices of the bearers of those objects. Chained immobile in the flickering firelight, they reach each other with their voices, and together they construct a conception of their world and a philosophy of their own. It is built only on shadows, but I think that is beside the point. At least they have each other.

Vera, who owned the Cave, had a good heart but took no shit from anyone. She tended bar on Friday and Saturday nights, when boys from Waterville State College came downtown to drink obscure Scandinavian or Dutch beer and she needed two bartenders to handle them and make sure they threw up *out-side*. Vera paid almost all the bartenders under the table with money from the cash register at the end of the night, plus the tips in the goldfish-bowl tip jar set prominently next to the cash register. Only Rafi and Vera herself were on the books—and then only as a strategy to avert the suspicions of the Internal Revenue Service. In addition to wages and tips, bartenders could help themselves to a pack of cigarettes from the rack be-hind the bar whenever they wanted and could drink free beer anytime, except supposedly not until after closing on nights when they were working. The cheapest beer was National Bo-hemian—called "Natty BoHo"—at seventy-five cents a can, but the bartenders, like royalty, drank two-dollar beer in bottles. People mostly tipped a quarter or thirty-five cents. Sometimes the bartenders would make change out of the tip jar just to get some folding money into it. When I got hired, Vera told me that if trouble—real trouble—ever broke out, the first thing I should do was grab the tip jar.

Despite Vera's precautions, the undeniably suspicious minimalism of Rafi's economic life did eventually draw the attention of the local IRS field office. After a series of written exchanges equally impenetrable on both sides, Rafi was invited to present himself to a man in a windowless office and explain how his claims of Thoreauian simplicity could possibly be true. He was instructed to bring receipts.

Rafi sat with a shoebox full of little scraps of paper on his lap while the IRS man, with the usual contempt of the barely middle class toward those they suspected of harboring bohemian tendencies, slowly and thoroughly established that Rafi, indeed, had no other income, no car, no mortgage, no savings account, no retirement account, no stocks or bonds, no life insurance, no real or personal property of any significant value at all.

"Don't you own *anything*?" the IRS man yelled finally, halfway between despair and disgust.

"Well," Rafi said after some thought, "I have a baseball glove that was signed by Mickey Mantle."

This was true, but it made the IRS man so indignant that Rafi was audited every year for eight years in a row until finally one audit showed he had overpaid his taxes by almost forty dollars, which was eventually refunded to him by government check, and after that he never heard from them again.

If you went out the back door of the Cave, you could go either right or left along the alleyway past the closed back doors of the drugstore and the record store and a store that sold area rugs. Or if you went straight ahead, you could thread your way along a narrow passageway and come out on Thornapple Street and be standing next to a Mexican restaurant called Tia Tortilla's that also had a bar. In those days, state laws were such that establishments could serve hard liquor only if at least 51 percent of their receipts were for food. It was always a near thing at Tia's, where the pork dishes in particular were a little suspicious. To make the 51 percent quota, shots of tequila sometimes had to be rung up as French fries. Without 51 percent in food, bars could serve only beer and wine. The Cave served only beer, although years before I arrived someone had once brought back two single-serving screw-top bottles of airplane wine from a long vacation. They were kept in a special place behind the bar in case of emergency.

Because of the proximity, regulars went back and forth between the Cave and Tia's many times during the course of the evening, so that the two bars almost felt like one. You couldn't pay your tab from one in the other, but the bartenders in Tia's would let you carry a water glass with two fingers of tequila in the bottom back to the Cave to buck up the bartender there if it looked like it was going to be a long night.

Some regulars—especially the older ones who were troubled by their aches and their livers and were, therefore, somewhat sour of disposition—moved only once in the evening, from the Cave to Tia's when the bands started up at the Cave. They hated to have to do it because there was no seventy-five-cent beer at Tia's. Every now and then, an especially stupid customer would complain about the noise to Vera. We never had one stupid enough to complain to Vera twice.

Hank and Stinky wanted to complain but didn't have the nerve to do any more than grumble behind Vera's back. "Vera," they would snort to each other with lots of conviction and very little volume, "she has *no idea* how to run a bar."

"If *I* ran this place," they would say, puffing out their chests to each other, "it would sure be different." Then they would deflate and glance around nervously.

Hank was a big man with a big belly that poured over his big silver belt buckle and a big walrus mustache almost long enough to meet his sideburns down low on a stubbly chin. Stinky was tallish and skinnyish and tightly wound, with a little toothbrush mustache and a little pointy goatee. Hank was losing his hair and opted for the traditional stringy comb-over, which he kept well plastered down. Stinky was losing his hair, too, but went instead for a three-quarter-inch buzz cut all around that made him look like a cue ball dressed up for Halloween as a hedgehog.

Stinky's real name was Jefferson Davis Smithfield Jr. He tried to get everyone to call him "J. D.," but instead we called him "Stinky" because we could come up with no other explanation for his perpetually pinched-up look. We had numerous theories of what had crawled into his mustache and died, but none of them could ever be proven.

Hank had an invisible wife who, Lord knows, did not mind at all how many hours he spent sitting in the Cave. Stinky was divorced and had gone twice now to Thailand, where he apparently enjoyed the company of a very young prostitute who said her name was Mary and who assured Stinky that although, of course, she occasionally knew other men, her relationship with him was different; he was the only one she truly loved.

Even Hank was skeptical.

Stinky would protest and bluster. It *was* different. She *did* love him. *He* was a real man, the only man. The best lover ever. She meant it. None of us pathetic losers could even begin to imagine the delights they tasted during the long, neon-lit, paid-by-the-hour tropical nights, the soft breezes, the palm trees rustling and the full moon glowing right outside the whorehouse door.

"I dunno, Stinky," Rafi said once, wiping up a wet patch on

the bar. "It seems like an awful long way to go just to get laid."

"Shows what you know, my friend," Stinky said. "I don't know why I waste my time even *trying* to elucidate certain facts for personages such as yourself who clearly lack the mental insight to even conceive of what I'm talking about. I'm telling you that this girl is special. The problem with you is that you have no sophistication."

"I dunno, Stinky," Rafi said again, shaking his head. "Maybe so."

Across Thornapple Street from Tia Tortilla's was a little yellow house that was the Hammer and Sickle Bookstore, run by Commie Tom. After two separate home-repair do-it-yourselfers were sadly disappointed during his first week of business, Commie Tom hung a big poster of Che Guevara in the front window, complete with beret and inspirational quote ("Better to die standing than to live on your knees"), and that seemed to clear everything up. Despite the death quote, this was not in any way a gesture of hostility. Commie Tom was sincerely concerned about the inconvenience he inadvertently caused people who were trying to buy hammers. He hated for people to be disappointed. He did add a small selection of home improvement books next to the Critical Race Theory section, just in case.

It was a pity, in a way, that those people no longer stumbled into the store because Commie Tom dearly loved converting the masses, joyfully pouncing on the unredeemed. When I think of him now, I remember him laughing in delight while his cat, Emma Goldman, chased a yarn ball tied to her tail, spinning madly across the bookstore floor. Tom would put on a tape of whirling dervish music, get Emma Goldman going, and sit on the floor and roar.

Tom handled the inherent conflict between being a communist and being a business owner by mostly giving away the stock. In fact, it was tricky to get Tom to sell you a book, to get him to take your money for it.

"Tom," you would start off, "I've been wondering about the oppression of diamond miners in South Africa," or whatever.

"Oh, yes, yes!" Tom would say. "That is so fascinating! I've just been reading a really excellent book about that. Now where did I put that? I just saw it. It's right here somewhere." And off he would go, rummaging through half the store, ending up with fourteen different books you should read, piling them one by one in your arms. "Oh, you *have* to read this. And the companion volume—very trenchant analysis. An interesting twist on commodity fetishism—you'll appreciate it. Take this one, too. Oh, and this!" Until finally the long-sought diamond-mining book appeared from where it had been mislaid in the Lesbian Poetry section. "Aha! I *knew* I had it here somewhere. Take this and let me know what you think about it. Oops—and this one, too. No, no, don't pay—just bring them back when you're done. No, if you want to keep them—if you're really sure—you can pay me later. I just want to see what you think of them first. We'll talk when you've read them, no hurry. Here, let's put those in a box. Any interest at all in the ancient Greeks? I ended up with three dozen copies of Edith Hamilton's *Mythology*—I'm sending the covers back to the publisher, but you take the book. I also have *The Dialogues of Plato*, but only volume two. Look, I'll just pack it right in your box here on the side. *Oof!* This box is heavy! You can't lift that—let me carry it to the car for you. No, no, no trouble at all!"

He was like that with everybody, even Republican evangelical Christians who went into the store just to try to get his goat. I saw it.

Twice Commie Tom almost lost the bookstore to the bank. He was a terrible capitalist. If some of the left-leaning professors at Waterville State College hadn't bypassed the university bookstore and made their students buy copies of expensive textbooks they ordered only from Tom, I don't know how he could have survived. The professors helped him because of a generous feeling toward little bookstores and a selfish feeling that if they ever wrote a book themselves, Tom would put it on display right on the front counter and would even try to sell some before he started giving them away.

Quite often, Tom came by the Cave in the early afternoon and drank coffee. We never charged him for it. Of course, we never charged anybody. This was because nobody but Tom and the bartenders ever drank the coffee, which was inexplicably greasy and tasted like bug spray for days after the exterminator made his regular, albeit futile, visits. The bartenders drank the coffee to steady their nerves first thing in the day. Tom walked past the entrances to two actual restaurants (Tia's and a little café called the Fiddlehead Fern, which I hardly ever went into because it was only open during the daytime) to drink greasy, bug-repellent coffee with the Cave bartenders. He even had a coffeemaker in his own store. I have no idea what was wrong with him.

The best times were after last call, when the last of even the regulars were gone and the band was packing up and the bartender was restocking all the coolers with beer for the next day. We would carry the trash cans to the dumpsters out back and heave them up and tip them over the side so the empty glass bottles slithered out all at once in a riotous, shattering cascade that sounded like the clanging cacophony of cathedral bells. It was strangely beautiful music in the still night air.

The Cave was never really empty after closing. Besides whoever was tending bar and whoever was left from the band, Vera would be there to count up the money and make out the deposit slip to go into the bank bag. And the bartender from Tia's was there because it was more friendly to have a nightcap with everyone at the Cave than to have it all alone over at Tia's, where the big plate-glass front windows invited unwelcome surveillance from bored policemen.

There were some people who were always welcome to sit in the premises after closing and drink a free beer and smoke free cigarettes, even though they had no connection of any formal kind with the Cave. These were people who had struck Vera's fancy, or Rafi's, or who were generally known and acknowledged as being "good people" who wouldn't cause trouble in any way or be jackasses. Or at least not very often.

Pancho the piano tuner was always welcome to stay after hours. It was hard to tell whether Pancho was an old man who seemed young or a young man who seemed old. He had played honky-tonk piano at bars and smoky concert halls all around the state ever since he was way too young to be in those kinds of places. He had discovered whiskey at ten, heroin at fifteen, and Jesus at twenty-one. Now his wild black hair was starting to have threads of gray and his eyes, which often seemed to be looking at something no one else saw, were crinkled with crow's-feet. He had enough rough road behind him now not to be shocked or bothered by other people's foibles, which led many of those same other people (if their particular foible was meanness) to assume that Pancho was stupid.

Every now and then, Pancho would come by in the afternoon and tune the battered upright piano that stood against the wall next to the dartboards in the little cleared space where the bands played. This was not an easy job (especially if people were playing darts) because players did terrible things to that piano, like putting metal thumbtacks into the hammers to make it sound more like they imagined Jelly Roll Morton's must have sounded when he played ragtime in the Storyville whorehouses a hundred years ago. It took ages to undo. After he got all the tacks out, Pancho would tune the piano with his eyes closed. We would try to be quiet while this was going on but didn't really need to be. Pancho could tune the piano even while the radio was on. He didn't hear anything else.

During the periods when the piano had been recently tuned and was still in pretty good shape, Pancho would sometimes play it after hours. He never played honky-tonk then, even though he still did occasionally around town with bands that needed a fill-in. Instead, for us, he played Beethoven sonatas, things like that. I didn't know what they were, but they made me think of nighttime or mourning doves or tangled primeval forests.

"What *is* that, Pancho?" I asked him once.

"Old men will have dreams, Josie," he said, and smiled. And that is all I ever got out of him.

ORIGINS

IN *SYMPOSIUM*, PLATO RECOUNTS Aristophanes's theory of the origin of Love.

In the beginning, Aristophanes says, there were three types of humans. These beings had two faces (one on either side of their heads), four arms and four legs, four ears, and three complete sets of genitalia. One type was all male, one type was all female, and one type was both male and female. Whenever these first humans wanted to run, they could put down all their limbs and turn cartwheels in any direction like whirligigs. They were fast and powerful and caused no end of trouble to the gods. On one occasion, the humans even attempted an assault on Olympus itself. They were a race with ambition to conquer the heavens and perhaps the power to do it.

Disturbed by the developments on earth, Zeus called a council of the Olympians to come up with a way of controlling these troublesome upstarts. Together the gods devised a plan to ensure that humans would never again have the wherewithal to challenge the gods. One night, Zeus went to earth with his blinding lightning bolts and split each of the humans into halves, severing them apart, dooming us each forever to incompleteness. He hid the terrible wound that this left, but he did not heal it.

Ever since then, bereft halves have spent their lives roaming the earth, searching for that other half who will complete them. Loneliness is the punishment for ambition.

Aristophanes says that we wrap our arms and legs around each other, we make love with each other, futilely trying to join again the pieces Zeus split apart. We are always searching for that *one*—the single other wanderer who belongs to each of us and completes us—because he was part of us in the beginning of time.

By the time I managed to leave home, to get out of the Smoky Mountains where I was born and raised, I was pretty sure my other half wasn't anywhere up there. There wasn't anyone— anything—for me.

In the summer, with the windows open in the house where I grew up, it was easy to hear the conversations the adults were having. Lying in bed at night, the air hot and still with the grown-ups' voices murmuring through the darkness, I could hear everything they said, even if they whispered.

"I'd be glad to have Belle stay all summer," Mama was saying to her sister, my aunt Sis, about beautiful Belle, my cousin.

"Just 'til I get back on my feet," Aunt Sis said. "I hope she won't be too much trouble."

They were talking in the kitchen, drinking cups of Nescafé. I could smell it in hot little bursts whenever they poured boiling water onto another spoonful of crystals.

"Oh, Belle is never any trouble," Mama said. "I like having her here, to tell you the truth. It's nice to have a girl around to do for. Do girl things for, I mean."

Aunt Sis laughed. "Josie's a girl," she said.

Mama laughed, too. "Not hardly."

I was named for Uncle Joe. He taught me how to shoot, practicing on beer cans balanced on the top rail of the fence out back of his house in the woods. The first shot knocked me backward off my feet, but Uncle Joe didn't laugh at me, just helped me up and dusted me off some.

"You'll do better next time," he said.

So the next shot, I tried to be strong. I didn't hit my target, but I stayed on my feet.

"That's the ticket," Uncle Joe smiled.

Later on, he looked worried and said to me, "Now you don't need to tell your mama anything about all this out here. She'd burn my biscuits good if she knew what I was letting you do."

"Mama says I ought to be more ladylike, stop running so wild," I told him. "Do girl stuff."

"Like what?"

"I don't know—whatever girls do, I guess."

"Oh, not yet, Josie," he said, still looking worried. "Not for a while yet."

As I got older, I learned more. I learned to listen like I was interested when boys talked about cars and when girls talked about boys. I learned never to let on when I read a book. I learned you should never get into a car with a boy who was a member of the National Athletic Brotherhood unless you were prepared to fight your way out. I learned never to let a boy I liked know I was a better shot than he was. I learned to keep my plans of leaving to myself.

🍺

The cable TV channel out of Atlanta showed Atlanta Braves baseball games and colorized movies. Sometimes those two worlds collided and there were movie stars in the stands at the baseball games. The camera would show them sitting there in their Atlanta Braves baseball hats and T-shirts and their designer sunglasses, looking intense and cool.

I thought to myself that it must be really something to live in a city like Atlanta and go to baseball games with movie stars. Or go to any big city where there were things to do that I'd never done and people to meet who didn't already know me. I could get a job there or maybe go to college someday. It would be better, anyway, than living at home with Mama and going nowhere and doing nothing. Somewhere outside those mountains was a world that was colorized.

When I was fourteen, I started waiting tables at the combination fish fry and gas station Uncle Joe ran out on the county line. I saved all my tip money, hidden in a coffee can in the shed. Every dollar was another step down the road to a bigger world.

🍺

The day after my twenty-first birthday, I arrived in Waterville on the bus with one suitcase filled with all my worldly goods, the contents of the coffee can, and a four-hundred-dollar loan from Uncle Joe. ("But it's all your savings," I said when he pressed the cash into my hand. "Maybe you'll need it for college someday," he said. "Wouldn't that be something?" "I can't take it," I said. "Pay me back when you can," he said.)

I went into the coffee shop of the Greyhound station and bought a Coke, more to give myself time to get my bearings than out of thirst. A man was sitting at the counter reading a newspaper while a little boy next to him alternately looked out the windows at the bus parked by the curb, took drinks from a tall glass with a straw, and spun his stool around and around.

"You came on the bus," the little boy said to me.

"Yes," I said.

"Did you sit behind the driver?"

"No, I sat kind of in the middle."

"I'm going to drive the bus someday."

"Are you?"

"Not today, though. Right?" He looked up at the man next to him for confirmation.

"Not today," the man smiled down at him. "Today we're just looking."

"Just looking," the little boy repeated while he spun his stool again. "Let's go look outside now."

"Okay," the man said, and folded the newspaper. He left it on the counter when he got up.

"Do you mind if I look in your paper?" I asked the man. "I need to find a job and a place to stay."

"All yours," the man said.

The little boy had hold of his hand and was tugging him out the door. "Come on, Rassi," he said.

"Good luck," the man said somberly to me. "I'm sure you'll find something."

I spent the next hour circling ads and found a place to live that very day. It was three rooms down by the river, with weeds out front and mud out back. The rent was a hundred dollars a month. I figured I'd be able to get some waitress work pretty soon. But I didn't find a job until after I ran into Rafi again, started hanging around with him, and went to work in the Cave.

There were maybe some possibilities for finding my other half in that town, I thought.

♥♥♥

Rafi had no girlfriend to speak of then, which was odd because he had dark wavy hair and hands that were both strong and delicate looking. His hands would shake some, though, before he had his first drink of the day, and that may have had something to do with the unsettled nature of his love life. Every February, he gave up drinking for the month and was, as a result, especially melancholy. He said he did it because he wanted to know that he could, but he picked February because it is the shortest month. Leap years were always particularly tough.

There were only two people I think Rafi loved.

The little boy I first met him with was Jordan. He was four—Rafi's sister's son. Despite Rafi's bartender's hours, quite often when he arrived at work, he had spent the morning with Jordan.

"Pumpkin Head and I saw a new calf today," Rafi would say, carefully avoiding my eye so I wouldn't see the punch line coming. " 'Look, Jordan,' I said, 'it's a new baby cow. It's just been born today. Today is its birthday.' 'Oh, Rassi.' " Here Rafi would imitate Jordan's droll, deep-voiced baby talk, wagging his head in baby resignation. About half of Jordan's sentences started, "Oh, Rassi," and were accompanied by a small, patient sigh. " 'Oh, Rassi. It cannot be that cow's birthday. How can it have a birthday if it cannot open the packages and cannot play with the toys?' " Then Rafi would look sideways at me, and I would laugh for him.

"I saw Pumpkin Head today," Rafi said, filling the cash register with change from the bank bag. "He had this little fire truck that was supposed to have lights and a siren, but it wouldn't work.

" 'Let me see if I can fix that truck for you there, Jordan.'

" 'Oh, Rassi, you cannot fix that truck. A wire is broke.'

" 'Are you sure, Jordan? Maybe it just needs new batteries.'

" 'It is not batteries. It a wire, Rassi. It a wire.'

" 'Well, maybe not. How long has it been broken?'

" 'Oh, Rassi, the weeks go on and on.' "

▉▉▉

Rafi didn't drive, or at least he didn't have a car. I'm not sure of any particular reason for this, but it was probably a good decision. So Rafi had to live no farther than walking distance from work. At one point, a patron gave him an old Stingray bicycle that he rode for a while, but then something untoward happened on his way home in the dark one night, he limped for about a week, and the bicycle was never seen again.

Rafi shared a tiny white frame house with a carpenter named Billy Joe, who was the best guitar player I ever heard in person. As a young man, Billy Joe had lived in Memphis and had once cut a demo tape in a studio there. By a long chain of good luck and kindness, one of Elvis Presley's Memphis Mafia— the one named Landon—heard the tape and liked it and called Billy Joe on the telephone. "Son," Landon said to Billy Joe, "we're going to make you a star." He invited Billy Joe to come to Grace- land sometime soon. But the very next day, Elvis was found face down, dead on the bathroom floor, and Billy Joe never went to Graceland but instead came back home and played the Cave pretty regular.

The white frame house was set back from the road at the end of a dirt drive, dwarfed by giant oak trees and hidden by scrub. Amenities in the house were somewhat scarce, and there was enough furniture outside and enough mice inside to make the distinction between being outdoors and being indoors a pretty fine one. The door we all used led straight into a kitchen that had a table with three chairs and an old stove with an iron skillet full of smooth river stones sitting on the back left burner. Rafi and Billy Joe said they were waiting until the stones were done to move out of the house.

Early on, Danny took me to a place he knew of—a barbecue shack out on the old blacktop highway toward Millboro. It had weathered board walls and tobacco farmers sitting with their wives and kids at the little tables, drinking sweet tea. There was no menu, and no one needed one. Danny and I ate plates of barbecue with slaw and hush puppies and drank cold beer.

"This is extra-special barbecue, sugar," Danny said. "This is the barbecue I grew up on."

We sat close together, and I could feel the warmth coming off his arm close to mine. I could hardly eat for thinking about what it was like to kiss him—I had just been kissing him that afternoon. I lowered my voice to talk to him under the restaurant sounds, so he would have to lean nearer to me to hear what I said.

"Good Lord, Danny, this is nearly a whole pig I've got here—I'll never in a million years finish it all."

"Eat up, sugar. You never know when you might need your strength."

"I'll bust!"

"Let me help you out with some of those hush puppies, then."

He put his arm across the back of my chair and ate off my plate. I held my icy beer bottle to my face, hoping it would cool me off. After he ate my hush puppies, Danny ate my barbecue and my slaw, too. I drank cold beer and watched him.

When he was finally done, he said, "Sugar, I'm stuffed. My belt's so tight it's cutting off all my important circulation. You're gonna have to drive back."

"Silly boy, you'll make yourself sick."

"I'm glad I brought you here," he said.

"Because I let you eat my dinner?"

"Because it's someplace I've never taken anybody else since I was a kid, and I knew you'd like it."

"I haven't said I like it."

"But you do—I can tell you do."

"Yes," I said. "I do. I like being here with you."

We paid the bill and bought two more bottles of beer to take home with us.

When state government officials set up the laws regulating the public sale of alcohol (concerned with the moral turpitude and degeneracy associated with alcohol consumption, but not averse to a short stiff one themselves, should the occasion arise), they decreed that all bars should close no later than 1 A.M. They decreed this in the winter. But as everyone knows, the workings of daylight saving time mean that 1 A.M. in the winter is 2 A.M. in the summer. So when the time changed in the spring, the bars all started staying open until 2 A.M. The bartenders from then on greeted Spring Forward, when the late shift got an hour longer, with mixed emotions. Summertime was better if you were doing the drinking, but not so much if you were doing the bartending.

Spring Forward always happens on a Saturday night, and Vera told me that every year the Friday night before that—the last night of early closing—was the night of the secret Bartenders' Ball.

Being below ground and consequently windowless, the Cave provided the perfect location for activities that were not strictly in keeping with Alcoholic Beverage Control regulations. The routine was that you were not to park your vehicle anywhere near the Cave, so the police would not see a big herd of cars all together on the street and feel morally obliged to investigate. You walked to the Ballroom Entrance of the Cave and pounded on the door. Vera would yell, "We're closed!" and then you would say who you were, and Rafi would let you in.

The night of that year's Bartenders' Ball, I got there first. That was because I was already there, having been sitting at the bar for hours keeping Rafi and Vera company and watching a band called Attention K-Mart Shoppers, made up of ironic English majors, play to an empty room and then disconsolately pack up and wander away. Vera and Rafi were busy restocking the coolers and locking up the money because although we loved our friends, we thought it best not to tempt them. Rafi's kind, weary face was beautiful in the glow of the red light bulbs, leaning over the coolers, filling them with Natty BoHo.

It is always awkward to be the first at a party, and I tried to look busy and entertained by smoking a lot of cigarettes, but it was rough going, so I was glad when Pancho sidled in, sat down next to me, and told me he had bought a watermelon that afternoon, which was unusual for that time of year and which gave us a topic of conversation while we waited.

The party started slowly, the bartenders who were off that night slipping in and diffidently depositing a bottle of vodka or tequila onto the bar and then shuffling down toward the dartboards. Next came the wait staff from the restaurants downtown, then the busboys, then the cooks and dishwashers, smelling strongly of detergent and steam. When Billy Joe showed up, he was carrying his guitar and leaned the case against the wall by the piano, which seemed quite natural but also quietly exciting, in a promissory kind of way. The last to arrive were the bartenders coming off the late shift uptown, who had finally closed up. When Vera told them we were closed, everyone said their names except for Commie Tom, who shouted, "The workers control the means of production!" and was greeted with loud cheers upon entering.

Like most people, the best music I've ever heard has been played on front porches or in kitchens or late at night when I least expected it. (I remember sobbing like my heart would break at 3 A.M. on I-40 in the Texas Panhandle over a song that came on the radio that I had never heard before and have never heard since.) That night, the music at the Bartenders' Ball was no different, unexpected and heartbreaking in the early-morning hours.

When Billy Joe finally started playing, it was just him and Pamela, a coolly beautiful and efficient waitress from a café uptown, sitting back to back on the piano bench, leaning together, Pamela singing the blues in a deep, slow way that made you stop what you were doing and wonder why you'd never heard her sing before. A whole crowd of busboys left off their pool games in the back room and came up front near the bar to listen. Eventually Pancho nudged Billy Joe up from the piano bench, and

Billy Joe didn't miss a note. Lanky Charlie Blue, the dishwasher from Tia's who had never played in public, brought in a doghouse bass from his truck on Thornapple Street. A girl called Rosalita who worked part-time at the Hammer and Sickle sang harmony with Pamela with her eyes closed, and three waiters from the Fiddlehead Fern were slapping out the rhythm with their palms on the bar. Vera was dancing, a sight I thought I'd never see. Rafi grabbed me tight, and we spun down the whole length of the room.

Later on, things got out of hand—which was the point, after all—although no real damage was done, other than that one of the busboys from Tia's finally lost his virginity and someone drank both bottles of screw-top airplane wine.

There are three things I especially remember about that particular Bartenders' Ball. The first is that I ran into Commie Tom by the pool tables and said, "Hey, Tom, what's up?"

"I'm getting drunk and making an ass out of myself," he said.

"What're you doing that for?"

"*Ahhhh.*" He opened his arms wide with an expansive smile like a saint. "It keeps you young! Nothing makes you feel fifteen years old again like waking up in the morning and realizing you've completely embarrassed yourself in front of all your friends."

The second thing was that Stinky tried to get in and Vera wouldn't let him, and we found out later that he'd gone home and gotten a dozen eggs and come all the way back and egged her car.

The third thing was that I met a man named Danny, whom I had never seen before, and when I woke up late the next day, he was asleep in my bed.

♆♆

DANNY

PLATO TELLS US THERE ARE OTHER PEOPLE in the cave, walking between the prisoners and the fire behind them. He doesn't say who these people are or where they come from—only that they pass back and forth behind the prisoners carrying objects that cast shadows on the walls in front of the prisoners. They talk to each other, and the sounds they make echo through the cave. They never communicate with the prisoners or try to help them or seem to notice them at all.

Plato doesn't say it directly, but these people must be the gods of the cave world. They are inexplicable and aloof, but they know a reality that the prisoners do not. The prisoners believe that the shadows they see are solid and that the echoes they hear have meaning. Only the "gods" know that the shadows are an illusion. They alone know it is their own voices that are the source of the echoes.

But although the gods have knowledge, they do not have control. For the prisoners are, in a way, free. The prisoners can spin a whole world out of shadows and echoes—a world they make among themselves, a world they conjure from their own imaginings, a world without limits, if only they can think it. Here the prisoners are free to invent infinite dreams and glorious theories. Anything is possible.

Meanwhile the gods tread back and forth on their walkway, bearing their burdens in the gloom. It is difficult to tell sometimes who is really a prisoner.

The first time I saw Danny, at the Bartenders' Ball, he was fighting with Vera—not physically fighting, because Danny always said it was beneath him to hit a drunk, but arguing loud and long enough that there was a little cleared space around the two of them and the people nearest to them were eyeing each other and looking skittish.

"Do you think we should do something?" I asked Rafi.

Rafi was sitting on the bar, where he could help himself to beers without having to get up.

"Do something?" he asked, like I was crazy. "*Do* something?"

"Do you think Vera needs help?" I asked, a little chagrined.

Rafi almost laughed. "Vera can take care of herself."

Around dawn, people started to leave in ones and twos, stepping outside into the fresh morning air and breathing deep to clear their heads before going to bed. The sky, glimpsed through the opening ballroom door, was indigo, then gray, then suddenly rose pink. Billy Joe was among the last to leave, taking Rafi and also a pretty blond girl with him in his car back to their house. I bolted the front door closed behind them before I started to restock the coolers.

Vera was shooting pool in the back room, and even though

I shouldn't have been, I was surprised when I went back there to find her laughing with the same boy she'd been fighting with earlier. Vera was always partial to people who gave as good as they got. They were playing nine-ball, and she was whipping his ass.

I should say right now, so you get the sense of him, that Danny was like whiskey held up to the light—warm and glinting. Even though we hadn't been introduced, he knew me already because Danny never met a stranger.

"Come shoot some pool with me, Josie," he said, all delighted to see me, like I was an old friend. "I'm losing bad, and there's five dollars on the line."

He was from deep in the country—born in Dogwood and raised in Millboro, an even littler town—and the way he drew out the word *five* was irresistible. I was half in love with him before he was halfway through. By the time he finally got to *dollars*, I was a goner.

"Come on, Jake," Vera said. "You and me against Danny and Josie—I could sure use the money." Vera was talking to a dark-haired man stretched out on a bench in the corner. We were the only four left in the bar.

The man called Jake was a stranger to me. He gave me a long, appraising look. "Ten dollars," he said, slowly getting up. I decided right then that I didn't like Jake too much.

By the time it was all over, Danny and I had lost forty dollars (almost entirely my fault) and kissed for a while up near the bar (almost entirely his).

Two doors down from the Hammer and Sickle on the corner of Thornapple Street and Magnolia was another yellow-painted house that was Blossom's restaurant. In the mornings, it opened at six-thirty or seven o'clock and was generally full of hardworking people already on their way to work or hard-living people finally on their way to bed. Either way, Blossom gave you what you needed—biscuits and gravy, eggs, country ham, grits, strong coffee. After Danny and I had lost beyond all redemption—his pool-playing reputation in shambles and mine sadly confirmed—we went over to Blossom's to eat. Vera yawned and said she was going home to bed, and Jake disappeared without saying goodbye.

Blossom was a large woman with a heart to match. She cultivated a loving attitude toward all of humanity and had six almost-grown children to show for it. They all worked in the restaurant, where the food was good and the use of butter plentiful.

Blossom had known Danny since he was a little boy. She, too, had grown up in Millboro and had come to Waterville years ago looking—like Danny was looking—for a wider horizon than tiny Millboro had to offer. She came over to our table with the pot of coffee.

"Baby," she said to Danny, "you look beat." In the daylight, his eyes were lined with translucent blue shadows.

"No, ma'am," Danny grinned at her. "Up all night and ain't half beat yet."

"Does your mama know how wild you are?"

"Not unless you go and tell her."

"He was such a *sweet* child," she said to me. "Singing in the choir at church like a little baby angel." She shook her head in mock despair. "Oh, he's turned out so *bad!*" And she smiled at him.

"What I need," said Danny, "is ham and biscuits."

"What you need," said Blossom, "is to be taken care of."

"Same thing," he said.

"That's true," she said, and went off to get our breakfast.

We ate for a long time and then went home together to my house.

*

Later in the afternoon, he woke up and came out to the front porch, where I was sitting with coffee and a hangover, smoking cigarettes and wondering if I should wake him up before I left for work. He seemed surprised to see me.

"Do you want some coffee?" I asked.

"No, that's okay. I'll get some at work."

"There's some frozen waffles we could toast for breakfast."

He shook his head, not quite meeting my eye. "I don't want to put you to any trouble," he said.

"It's no trouble."

"You're sweet"—looking at the floorboards of the porch—"but I've got to go now."

"Right away?"

He didn't answer but kissed me instead, too quickly, too hard, just off-center on my mouth. Then he was gone.

I sat on the porch letting the coffee get cold and tried to hold on to the feeling of his lips against mine.

*

"Good party," Tom said when I went into the bookstore Monday morning.

"Have you recovered?" I asked.

"Still feel like hell, but, you know, in a good way," he laughed. "How about you?"

"I met somebody kind of nice—a guy named Danny."

"I know Danny—he's a good guy," Tom said. "I've had some fun times with Danny. Some real fun times. Of course, after a while . . . "

"What? After a while, what?"

Tom grinned. "Ah, well. I don't want to speak ill of the dead."

"He's not dead!"

"Hmm. As much as he was drinking, he should be."

"What are you saying to me?"

"Danny's a good guy," Tom repeated. "He's a lot of fun—has friends everywhere. A lot of people like him. A lot of women like him."

"Good Lord, Tom! I'm not talking about marrying the boy. I just think he's nice, is all. We had a good time together."

"Just be careful, Josie."

I snorted.

"Well, I've never been one to put a damper on adventure—as long as you're sure you're going in with your eyes open."

"All I said was that I think he's *nice!*"

"He *is* nice. That's true." Tom paused. "But be careful you don't start expecting too much."

"Don't worry. I never expect anything," I lied.

♉︎

The next day, I was at the gas station buying cigarettes, a newspaper, and a Big Red soda when I saw him. Through the rippled plate-glass window between the signs for cheap oil and day-old hot dogs, I saw the back of his head, rumpled sandy hair, and a rumpled farmer-boy shirt. I saw the way his shirt stretched across his shoulders.

"Regulars?" the boy at the cash register said to me.

I just nodded because it's so hard to talk when you can't

breathe. From outside, I heard Danny's laugh.

"Three dollars even," the boy said.

I put my money on the counter and noticed I was sweating.

"Do you have a bathroom I could use?" I whispered, and he nodded toward a door in the wall by the cooler.

Inside the piss-and-industrial-soap-scented bathroom, I leaned my forehead against the cool door and listened to Danny's faint voice as he paid for his gas and a tamale.

"You're a brave man," the cash-register boy said to him, and I listened to Danny laugh again and say words I couldn't make out. I didn't come out of the bathroom until I was sure he was gone.

"Everything okay?" the boy said to me.

I wanted to say, *No, no, everything is not okay. Because I can't stop thinking about that boy. He's been inside my head for two whole days now, and visions of him won't let me alone. And my hands are shaky and my heart is beating ninety miles an hour just because I heard his goddamn voice. No, everything is definitely not okay.*

"Everything's fine," I said.

The key to the front door of the Cave was kept in a little hidden spot on the ledge above the door. This wasn't the *very* most secure place to hide something, but the patrons were not exactly masters of detection, and it worked well enough. I liked being able to let myself in early even when I wasn't working. I waited for Rafi to show up, sitting at the bar in just the light from the TV screen, everything all quiet around me, thinking and listening to the muted sounds from the street above.

Three days after the ball, Rafi was not surprised to find me already there.

"Hiding out?" he asked.

"It's way too quiet at my house."

"Come help me with the pool tables."

I trailed after him to the back room.

"I hate waiting," I said. "It seems like I've spent my whole life waiting."

"Your whole life hasn't been so long."

"It seems long," I said ruefully, "because of all the waiting."

"You could call him." Rafi said this too casually and didn't look at me because he was paying extraordinarily close attention to folding up the pool-table cover.

"You know I can't do that," I said.

"Why not?"

I sighed. "Too chicken, I guess," I said finally.

"What are you afraid of?"

I got down the box of chalk and put three little cubes on the edge of each table.

"I'm afraid of finding out that I was just another girl. I'm afraid he'll answer the phone and not be able to place me."

"He'll be able to place you."

"Or that I'll hear somebody else's voice in the background— some other girl."

"It could be his sister."

"Does he have a sister?"

"Not that I know of. I think he has some girl cousins, though."

"I think the best thing is probably for me just to put him out of my mind. Just move on, you know? Let's you and me fall in love, Rafi."

Rafi snorted. "I know too much about you mountain girls," he said. "I've heard you're all wild—go off with strangers you meet in bars."

"I'm insulted. We could get married in a lovely ceremony in

the bus station where we met."

"And name the babies Greyhound and Trailways?"

"We'd call them 'Grey' and 'Trey' for short. They're twins."

"A boy and a girl who looks like you."

"Oh, Rafi. I hate waiting."

"Don't worry. He'll call. I'd call if I were him."

"I think I need a beer," I said.

"I think you do. Come on—you're the first customer of the day."

Why do women—decent, kindhearted women—like bad men? Why, when looking for that perfect other half that Zeus split off from them, do women who read books and brush their teeth after every meal gravitate toward men who shave irregularly and drink too much and don't even own any bedsheets? I didn't know the answer to that question back then, only that nice guys made me want to take a step or two backward whenever they talked too much to me.

Now, after all these years, of course, the answer is clear to me: the problem with nice guys is that they will never break your heart. They aren't going to just up and leave you for some other girl, prettier than you and more fun. A girl like my cousin Belle.

A bad boy, now—well, you can *count* on him. Deep in your subconscious, you are certain that the very minute you fall good and in love with him, he'll announce that he's gotten the preacher's daughter—hell, the preacher's *wife*—pregnant, and can he borrow two hundred dollars to take her to Vegas? And you'll give it to him—through your tears, you'll write him out a check even if it means using your last dime.

And the reason—even though you don't know it yourself

and would think someone was crazy if they told it to you—is that you're relieved, actually. It turns out that you're not ready, just yet, to give up your freedom. Your unerringly bad taste in men knows, even if you don't, that there are more kinds of paradise than just happily-ever-after, and that happily-ever-after itself sounds close enough to death sometimes as to make no difference.

And so you have to play your hand carefully here—choose the wrong boy and you could end up with a guy so nice that you can figure out no reason not to say yes when he asks you to marry him, which he will soon enough. That's what nice guys do. Choose well and you can drown your sorrows in peace and tequila with a clear conscience. You don't want to get permanently caught up with your wrong half when your right half is somewhere out there, waiting for you. But there's nothing that says, in the meantime, your wrong halves can't show you a good time.

Within ten seconds of meeting Danny, I knew he was a bad boy and that, although my heart was in serious danger, my freedom was absolutely safe. Whatever he would be to me, he wasn't going to be with me forever, wasn't going to be the one who healed the wound from Zeus. He made it pretty clear, right from the start, that he had no interest in forever. When he left my house at sunset that first day, I figured I wouldn't hear from him again anytime soon.

◆◆◆

When I woke up a week later and opened my front door, a note that had been caught in the screen door fluttered down onto the porch. It was from Danny, offering to buy me another breakfast. I wondered then if maybe I had been wrong about him.

Early spring in the Piedmont can be bleak and wet, but as I stood there barefoot on the porch, holding that note, the world was a dazzling sunlit green, warm and promising. It didn't occur to me to do it at the time, but I probably should have kept that note. It might have been a talisman.

My second breakfast with Danny started at twilight and lasted until all the bars had closed. He came home again with me, without asking, knowing he was wanted.

I lay beside him in the ghost light before dawn, watching him sleep and memorizing the curved line of his upper lip, the flush of sunburned skin across his cheekbone.

I don't know if I'll ever see you like this again, I thought, and held my breath so as not to wake him.

MADNESS

IN HIS DIALOGUE WITH PHAEDRUS, Socrates argues that it is Love that causes madness. We love what is beautiful, Socrates says, and are entranced by it so that the gods enter our souls and remind us of the Beauty we knew before birth, the perfect Beauty that cannot exist here in the world of flesh. Here on the earth, we see only the shadows of Beauty and hear only the echoes. But before we were born, Socrates says, we had knowledge of the world above, and we saw there true Beauty, in all its glory.

Now, in this life, sometimes it happens that Love can open for us the memory of our time before birth, when we walked with Beauty. And that remembrance is so profound in its power that we are captured by it and turn our eyes on it, unwavering and obsessive, heedless of the world around us and of the opinions of our fellow human beings, who will think we are mad.

Socrates says that this madness is a gift from the gods, well worth the price of scorn from mortals. But it is madness all the same.

¶

Danny lived in an old green house called Boystown. I don't know who actually owned the house. Whoever it was clearly had a laissez-faire attitude with regard to irregularities and goings-on. In exchange, the tenants of Boystown had an equally relaxed attitude toward repairs, services, and basic amenities. There were locks on the doors, but the keys had been lost so many years ago that no one could remember a time when the locks had been used. This was general knowledge, and it was not unusual for the boys to wake up and find unannounced guests asleep on the broken-down living-room sofa or helping themselves to coffee in the kitchen—so much so that it was frequently a matter of conjecture as to who actually *lived* there and who did not.

Danny and I were eating chicken and biscuits at the kitchen table at 3 A.M. when Jake wandered through. Whether or not he was an official tenant was unknown.

"Hey," I said.

"Hey," he said, and smiled. I don't know if he was feeling friendlier toward me since the pool debacle or whether he was just resigned.

Danny's bedroom featured teetering piles of papers and books, including coverless copies of Hamilton's *Mythology* and *The Dialogues of Plato*, volume two, which I assumed, like mine, were gifts from Tom. Danny was careful to hook the door behind us from the inside. This seemed to me at the time to violate the whole free-access ethos of Boystown, and I didn't know why he did it. I found out at 4 A.M.

It is a startling thing to be woken up by someone screaming, "*Motherfucker!*"

Repeatedly.

In fact, the woman pounding on Danny's door at 4 A.M. seemed to have a vocabulary consisting almost entirely of the word *fuck* and variations on the word *fuck*. Oh, and *bastard*.

"Have you ever met Candy?" Danny whispered in the dark.

"I don't think you've mentioned her," I said.

"I didn't think so," he said, and then added after a pause, "She's sweet."

Through the door, we heard Jake's voice sounding firm but reasonable, as if faced with a wild animal that was considering biting him. His voice was low enough that we couldn't make out the words. But after a while, Candy seemed to calm down, and awhile after that we heard her car drive away. Jake knocked once on Danny's door.

"You owe me one," he said, and then went back to bed.

As it turned out, Candy and Danny had only very recently ceased to be a couple. Extremely recently. So recently, in fact, that it was possible Candy had not yet fully absorbed the news.

Two days later, after it had sunk in, she came back in the night and slashed Danny's tires.

♊

Stinky saw it as his solemn duty to lift us Cave dwellers out of the ignorance and delusion we wallowed in. And out of all us wallowers, Commie Tom, in Stinky's opinion, wallowed the most. Or at least he wallowed in the worst type of mud.

"Look," Stinky said, leaning down the bar toward Tom for emphasis, "you can't deny that there's a fundamental flaw right at the very heart of your whole ideological edifice. Put your whole head in the bag—right in!" (This last was said to Hank, who had a bad case of hiccups and was being run through a gauntlet of cures by Stinky.)

Tom smiled at Stinky in the benevolent way people have at the end of the second beer when the third one is just coming up from the cooler. "How's that, Stinky?" he said, and I could see the lines of his shoulders relax into the discussion. He put his foot up on the rung of the barstool next to him.

"Well, now, here's the basic premise of my argumentation," Stinky said, getting excited because someone was willing to talk to him about his theories, which was not always the case. "I think it's obviously clear to anyone who's given consideration to the point that communism just won't work, not operationally. It goes against human nature. Against the very core of human nature."

"Now tell me how you see that, Stinky," Tom said, offering Stinky a cigarette out of his pack.

"Clearly, communism implies and necessitates some degree of selflessness going forward," Stinky said, taking the smoke from Tom. "That is, some degree of man putting his own fundamental ontological interest aside." (To Hank: "Here, drink from the back side of this cup.") He paused to light his cigarette on the match Tom held out for him.

"I don't quite follow you there," Tom said, taking his first drink of the new beer.

"Well, it's fairly self-evident to any halfway observant personage that altruism doesn't exist. That's just a given at this point in time."

"Plenty of people give to charity—," Tom said.

"Tax write-offs. Pure self-interest. (Just keep drinking from the back side.)"

"—or just help out a neighbor."

"See, that just exemplifies my point," Stinky said, getting a little heated. "You help out your neighbor and, when you do, you make good and certain the rest of the neighborhood observes you doing it. Or hears about it, anyway. I've been reading some material about this topic—delving into the neuroscience of it. You see, it's all about reputation or self-regard—thinking good about yourself, what a good guy you are. Releases endorphins. But nine times out of ten, I'm telling you, you wouldn't even have utilized the behavior in the first place if you hadn't somehow been *socially* forced into a corner over it. Socially speaking. Ninety percent of the time, in my estimation, you were probably hiding in the living room with the curtains pulled shut and the television volume down as minimally as it can go, just to avoid that exact same neighbor always asking, always wanting something, always looking for a handout. That's just fundamental human nature. It's all there, already encoded in your neurons with endorphins. It's neurologically imperative to avoid people who don't optimize your own self-interest. It's a fairly proven data point in a lot of the literature I've been delving into."

"There might be some debate about that," Tom said. "There's some interesting stuff in anthropology—"

But Stinky cut him off. "I can't believe you'd be so gullible! Don't believe everything you read, my friend. You need to apprise what you read more carefully. Try to utilize your brain here. Try to follow my line of reasoning. We start from the proposition that no man wants to be miserable. No man wants pain, and every man wants to make his own life better going forward. We all agree on that, right?"

"Well, I'm not so sure," Tom said. He was sipping beer number three, and his eyes had a faraway look.

"Whatcha mean, you're not sure?" Stinky shouted, and a little fleck of spit shot out from his mouth. "Every man is out for himself! You've got to be able to conceive of that! No man *wants* to be miserable, for Chrissake! (Boo!)"

The *boo* scared Hank so much that he dropped his beer, and

we thought for a minute that this cure had finally worked, but then the hiccups started up again, just as bad as ever. Rafi wiped up the spilled beer with a towel.

"Buddha said desire is the source of pain," Tom finally said when the commotion died down. "He was probably right. But still, we don't get rid of our desires, it seems to me. We keep them close to us. Maybe like hidden treasures, buried but never forgotten. Is it that we can't get rid of our desires, or is it that we don't really want to?"

"You're drunk," Stinky said, slumping back onto his barstool.

"Moderately," Tom admitted.

"Try thinking about naked women," Stinky said to Hank.

"I never heard that one," Hank said.

"Me neither," admitted Stinky. "Maybe it won't cure you, but at least you'll be happy thinking about naked women."

There was a pause while we all thought about naked women. Hank hiccupped.

"I knew a woman once in Denver," Tom said. "She was a friend. I knew her husband, too, but she was the one who was my friend."

Stinky glanced at Tom out of the corner of his eye and grinned. "Dog," he said, and poked Tom with his elbow.

"No," Tom said. "It wasn't like that. I used to talk to her."

"Always a good first step," Stinky said, and poked Tom again.

"Her husband was a pretty fast-track corporate guy, and he was making his name then. He worked a lot, and she was on her own a lot."

"It's an old story, buddy." Stinky leered. "No need to explain to us. Lonely women are low-hanging fruit."

Hank hiccupped.

"She loved her husband," Tom said. "And then they had a baby, and she loved the baby and loved her husband even more.

When she talked about him, I could tell how much she loved him."

Stinky looked perplexed and a little disgusted. "So what happened?"

"Nothing. I moved to Chicago eventually. We lost touch."

Stinky snorted. "I am failing to see what in the *hell* this discourse is about."

"I remember this one time . . . ," Tom started, but then he stopped and didn't tell the story after all.

"Did you get any?" Stinky asked.

"Never even tried. It wasn't like that."

"Jesus H. Christ, man! Why didn't you just bang her on your way out of town? Her husband most likely never would have become cognizant of the situation. And even if he did find out eventually, you'd be long gone. Did she get obese or something postpartum?"

"What I'm trying to say," Tom said, "is that sometimes the longing is the best part, I think. Or a good part, anyway. Sometimes I would go places where I thought she might be and, I tell you the truth, I could hardly even breathe, thinking I might see her. Longing is a powerful thing."

"And so you're telling me you *liked* being miserable over some fat chick, and you never even got any?"

Hank hiccupped.

"I wonder where she is now."

"I dunno, man." Stinky shook his head. "All I can say is that if it had been me, I would have banged her but good on the way out of town. Even if I *was* a goddamn communist."

Hank hiccupped. "Me, too," he said.

The Bartenders' Ball, of course, came only once a year. The rest of the time, an average night after closing at the Cave was pretty quiet—a handful of people hanging around killing time until they could figure out a way to go to sleep. The bartender restocked the beer. Vera counted the money. Pancho sat at a table in the corner with a deck of cards, and as, one by one, we all finished what we were doing, we would join in the special Cave version of rummy. The rules became more complicated and byzantine as the night wore on. Some of them were: If someone discarded a six, the direction of play reversed. Every third three that was played, you had to change hands with the person whose birthday was closest to yours. If a Dolly Parton song came on the radio, you had to discard all the face cards in your hand. The people with scores in the middle at the end of the night had to buy shots of tequila the next day in Tia's for the high and low scorers. This was to discourage mediocrity.

Now that Danny and I were seeing so much of each other, he came after closing to the Cave from the café uptown where he worked tending bar, and sat with Pancho and Rafi and Vera and me and played rummy.

In the town around us, almost everybody was asleep. The two taxi drivers who parked their cabs at the corner of Camellia and Thornapple Streets dozed, stretched out in their backseats. The policemen nodded off behind the wheels of the cruisers over on Juniper Street. Clyde was finished with the after-last-call fried-chicken rush and yawned behind the cash register in his lonesome pool of light. The frat boys from the college were asleep on their backs, snoring in their beer-soaked beds. The waitresses from the uptown restaurants had gone home and taken off their shoes and rubbed their feet and let their dogs out and gone to bed. Blossom had two more hours to go before she had to get up and start making biscuits. Men with clear consciences dreamed next to their wives. By the light of the test pattern on the TV screen, lonely insomniacs stared at the familiar furniture of their bedrooms and listened to the crickets.

But the Cave dwellers stayed up until dawn, smoking cigarettes and playing cards until the nighttime vanished. The nighttime was somehow far too lonesome to sleep in.

In the blue morning light, Danny would fall asleep in my bed. With his eyes closed, he looked younger, though sometimes he frowned or stirred with uneasy dreams. And once he shouted "No!" so loudly he woke himself up, looking dazed. Later he told me he didn't know what he had been dreaming. I thought that maybe those dreams were the reasons he didn't like to sleep too much, but Danny never said anything about them to me, and I never asked again.

Socrates spends only half a sentence discussing the moment when one prisoner is freed from his chains in the depths of the cave. He says only that the prisoner is freed and is compelled—for the first time ever—to stand. Socrates does not tell us who it is exactly who frees and compels the prisoner. He does not tell us how this particular prisoner, out of all the company, is chosen to be the one who, against his own will, eventually becomes enlightened. Why this one from among his fellows?

Perhaps Socrates skims so blithely over this moment—which is, nevertheless, the turning point of the whole story—precisely because part of the point is that it could have been any of them. It is the effect of the journey upward toward the light, the effect of the sunlight itself—rather than anything particular about the person who takes the journey—that makes the difference. The faceless being who frees only one prisoner does so without regard for the virtue or the intelligence or even the willingness of the chosen one. It could have been any of them.

And yet that choice, made so carelessly as to be unworthy of comment by Socrates, will make all the difference to one poor prisoner. Without desiring it or deserving it or even understanding it, his whole world is about to be changed. His whole world is about to be destroyed.

Danny said he traveled "unencumbered," which meant in practice that he shed his possessions in an erratic but ongoing trickle wherever he went—lost hats, lost paychecks, lost library books and sunglasses and car keys. It wasn't long before his Durham Bulls T-shirt was behind my couch, his cigarette lighter on top of my refrigerator, and his shoes under my bed, abandoned or misplaced. But once a man's shoes live under your bed, no matter how haphazardly they are left there, it starts to seem that you are on no extended one-night stand, no passing fling. You start to think that maybe the two of you belong together. You get used to having him around—or at least having his things around.

Because sometimes Danny himself didn't come down to the Cave for a while and I wouldn't run into him anywhere around town. When he wasn't around, I would pretend to pay attention to what other people were saying and pretend I didn't notice he wasn't there and pretend I didn't mind. After about three days or so, though, missing him would get to be so bad that I might even find myself paying attention to Stinky talking, just to have something else to listen to other than every tiny sound outside on the street—just in case it turned out to be the sound of Danny's voice as he was coming in the door. I would become, after just a few days without him, weirdly attuned to the sound of his name. *Danny.* I became so incredibly alert to the sound of his name that I could hear it just in the way that another woman drew in her breath to speak. Before she even said his name, I knew she would. I could always tell because she had the same haunted look on her face that I saw in my own mirror. *Danny.*

So when two college girls from uptown poked their golden heads through the Cave's door in the early evening and squinted uncertainly into the gloom and the more diaphanous of the two said to her friend, "This is the place he comes," I knew right away who *he* was. I could tell she was looking for Danny just by the way she sat at the bar, posed on the barstool like a bright and delicate bird, reminding me of my cousin Belle. I thought of how Belle had once shown me how to pull my shoulder blades together when I sat. "Makes your belly smaller and your boobs bigger," she said, posing. I'd tried later to re-create her stance in the mirror, with little success.

Standing there in the gloom of the Cave, I lit a cigarette even though I already had one going. Sometimes it is practically impossible to smoke as much as you need to.

"Hi," they chirped at me, smiling wide smiles and shaking their sunshine-colored hair off their shoulders. "What imported beers do you have?"

I pointed sullenly to the list on the wall. They studied it intently, biting their lower lips in pretty indecision and twirling identical strands of hair around identical forefingers in unconscious unison. Then they both ordered the Mexican beer we all called *Orinada* (Spanish for "puddle of piss") for obvious reasons and asked me if we had any limes. We didn't.

I got their beers and opened them and then made change from their new twenty-dollar bills, feeling suddenly like a brunette troll in the world of blond fairies. I noticed how grubby my own hands looked, with the telltale beer-opening callus on my right forefinger, compared to their clean white skin and discreet manicures. I moved to the other end of the bar to be out of range of both their Love's Fresh Lemon perfume and their bubbly conversation. I didn't want to hear them say his name. *Danny.* I turned the TV on and *Jeopardy!* sprang to life. I turned up the volume, but even that couldn't erase the glowing expectation they had carried in with them and the consequent gloom that engulfed me. I picked up someone's coverless copy of *Mythology* from where it had been abandoned by the tip jar and tried to concentrate on the story of Hera's jealousy causing her rival, Io, to be turned into a heifer, seeing the justice of this more clearly than I ever had in the past.

It was a slow evening, and they stayed a long time, looking up every time the door opened, their bright expectancy dwindling slowly through uncomplaining patience into restlessness and then boredom to end, finally, in peevish snapping. It was perhaps unbecoming to them but was less grating on my nerves, at least, than the initial self-assured giggling had been. Finally, after a whispered conversation involving clearly mimed exasperation and much glancing and suppressed gesticulating in my direction, the more pert of the two leaned across the bar and rather peremptorily called me over from my glum little lair at the very farthest end of the bar.

"Look," she said without any pretty lip-biting at all, "there's this guy I met, and I heard he comes in here all the time." I steeled myself, hardened my face so I wouldn't betray anything at the sound of Danny's name. "Do you know a guy," she asked, "named Billy Joe?"

I felt my knees go a little bit weak, and it occurred to me then that she wasn't actually such a bad sort of girl after all. I frowned deeply and tried to look like I was thinking hard. "Never heard of him," I said.

"Come back soon!" I called cheerily after them as they disappeared out the door, waspishly bickering at each other.

Danny himself turned up much later that night with Jake, Charlie Blue, a black eye, and the laughing-eyed smile he always had after the tequila started to kick in.

"Hey, pretty girl," he laughed at me. "I sure am glad to see you. Where've you been hiding at lately?"

"*I've* been right here," I said, feeling petulant.

"Well, now, that's a shame," he said, "because you should've been with me. We've been having a pretty good time. You could've been having a good time, too. Don't you have any sense?" He grinned all lopsided at me across the bar.

"Some of us have to work," I said.

"It's a shame," he said again, shaking his head. "That's what it is—a crying shame. I mean, what with you being so pretty and all."

He sighed a big fake horse-sigh and tried to look sorrowful and failed, and I laughed.

"There were two girls in here earlier," I ventured as casually as I could, "and I thought they might have been looking for you."

"*Pretty* girls?" he asked, leaning closer across the bar.

"Maybe," I said.

"And there were two of them together, you say?"

"They looked like girls from the college—like maybe cheerleaders or something."

He leaned even closer. "Mercy! Two pretty cheerleader girls roaming around together looking for someone."

I was watching his face. "I thought they might be looking for you," I said again. "Couple of pretty blond girls out on the town."

He was so close to me now that he could whisper. "My, my. That *is* a shame, too, because to tell you the truth, I find that just at the moment here, I can't stop thinking about this one brown-haired girl."

Then he tugged a lock of my hair and pinched me on the arm and took away my cigarette to smoke himself.

Danny tended bar at a café uptown. It was clean and well lighted and as such seemed an alien land to the Cave dwellers, who all felt that we appeared to our best advantage in subdued lighting and standing in contrast to outrageous background filth. The café was not without its charms, though, such as drinkable coffee and a fully stocked bar open at 8 A.M. Also, the patrons seemed extremely unlikely to vomit on you or even near you. Even though the waitresses were all beautiful and friendly, Hank and Stinky never came around.

Neither did Vera or Rafi or even Pancho. I felt like a spy and maybe a traitor when I first went to see Danny, skulking in the door sideways and scuttling to a seat at the far end of the bar, hidden from sight by the gleaming chrome cappuccino machine. Jake sat with me. Jake often hung around when Danny was working, not talking much, sometimes reading a coverless book from Tom, sometimes just nursing a beer. I was happy to see him at the café because, among all the well-dressed, intimidating customers there, at least he was a face I knew, someone who wasn't a stranger.

Danny's bartending was a performance to be envied. He teased everybody, flirted with everybody, and made everybody feel like they were the only one, special to him and lucky.

I was driving down a two-lane highway once when I saw a man changing a tire by the side of the road, and in the five seconds he was in my sight, it was clear that he needed no help—he knew exactly what he was doing, exactly how to change a tire. And just as I passed him, he finished tightening the bolts and, without looking at it, twirled the lug wrench once in his hand—like a bored baton twirler—without even noticing what he was doing. In those five seconds, I fell in love with that man. I told this to Rafi and he understood what I was talking about right away.

"Oh, God, yes," he said. "Competence is so sexy."

Danny at work was like that—making conversation and drinks with casual grace. As a consequence, there were always one or two women sitting at the bar wearing too much perfume and leaning too far forward, intent on him, eager. I watched him slipping between their fingers, and he would catch my eye and wink at me. I wondered how many women he winked at in the course of a night.

I never, from the very first, intended to fall in love with him.

But I couldn't help it—I watched him mix a drink without ever looking at the bottle he was pouring from and I completely lost my mind.

SUMMER

IN *MENO,* PLATO DISCUSSES the myth of Persephone's return. The goddess Demeter had a daughter named Persephone who was of such rare loveliness and charm that Hades, the god of the underworld, fell in love with her. One day while Persephone was out gathering flowers in a field, Hades rose up out of a dark chasm in the earth and captured her and carried her away to his kingdom of the dead. Demeter, the goddess of grain and the harvest, was heartbroken. Bereft of her daughter, she mourned for a whole year, and during that time nothing grew on the earth—no fruit or grain or grapes for wine.

Finally the great god Zeus, fearful that all humanity would perish unless the grief of Demeter was assuaged, compelled Hades to relinquish his bride and return Persephone to her mother. Thus ended the year of cold and famine. Demeter's joy at seeing her daughter once again caused the flowers to blossom, the trees to put out their leaves, and the fields to grow green and lush in the warm summer sun.

Alas for Demeter, her happiness could not last. During the time of her captivity in the kingdom of the dead, Persephone had refused all food and drink—save, on the last day, one pomegranate seed. But eating that seed was her undoing. By the inexplicable rules of the gods, it meant that Persephone must always return to Hades. For one-third of each year, she must return to the underworld and reign there for a time as queen. So each winter, Demeter mourns again the loss of her daughter, and the earth mourns with her, brown and sere and lifeless. But with the return of Persephone every spring, Demeter brings back the golden sunlight, the lush fields, the abundant fruitfulness of life.

If the Greeks are to be believed, we are not happy because it is summer—it is summer because we are happy.

Danny didn't usually operate on a regular schedule, and the lengths of his days and nights were erratic at best. Sometimes the phone rang at two o'clock in the morning or three o'clock or four.

"Hey, sugar. What took you so long to answer?"

"Um, I was asleep."

"Asleep? You don't want to be asleep now, sugar—you should see the moon tonight. It looks close enough to touch."

"But I'm trying to sleep!"

"Well, couldn't you come out with me to see the moon for just a little while, and then you could go to sleep later and I would go with you?"

Long pause.

And then Danny said, "We shouldn't waste the moon, you know. There may not be one when we get to hell."

From my bedroom window, we could still see the moon as it

set at dawn, translucent white in the colorless sky. Summer was just beginning then. The birds were stirring on the branches of the mimosa trees on Thornapple Street. Long shadows still lay across the grass, and the tiny pink and white daisies hadn't opened yet but just showed their tight little buds reaching above the grass from their thread-thin stems. The sun rose slowly over the hedges and the japonica bushes and came through the open bedroom windows in long, slanted streaks, and the air was getting warmer already. The birds became a full-fledged riot outside.

After a while, we slept. And then later on, when the afternoon air was still and heavy like wet silk and the birds were silent in the summer heat and only the heartbeat pulse of the katydids let us know the whole rest of the world hadn't vanished—then Danny kissed me goodbye, his face rough now with beard and the smell of him mixed with the smell of me. He kissed me and left, and I was alone in the heavy air and the katydids' song.

Looking back now, it seems to me that Demeter's joy suffused that whole summer. Vera, after years of cynicism, suddenly got all dreamy-eyed about a man named Pete. We used to keep a suspicious eye on Pete when he first started coming around the Cave because he looked like he probably knew more about the business end of things than we could even imagine. That was true, as it turned out, but it didn't stop him from also being sweet natured and honest and decent. He and Vera took to each other, appreciating a toughness born of necessity and a tenderness earned the hard way.

Commie Tom upped Rosalita's hours to full time and stopped coming by the Cave to drink coffee in the afternoons.

Instead he and Rosalita sat on the front porch of the bookstore and had long, long talks while customers inside helped themselves. Overheard snatches of conversation seemed to indicate that they had moved past the political situation in Central America and the fate of the American Indian Movement in the post-Peltier age and were now discussing whether or not it would be decadently bourgeois to open a joint bank account. She gave him a wallet with a picture of Karl Marx on it for his birthday, and he added a whole section of books on natural childbirth and baby care.

Even Pancho seemed more mysterious and smiled a lot to himself and was seen at the edge of town picking wildflowers.

That summer, I was fearless. This is the prerogative of the young. Later in life, you might have courage, which means doing things in spite of your fears. But never again will you really be without fear—flying above the world in wind-swept delight, close and closer to the sun, heedless of everything that lies below. Maybe it is only ignorance, but it has a remarkable resemblance to immortality, while it lasts.

On afternoons when Danny was working, sometimes I sat at a little table up against the wall of the café and pretended to read a paperback book. But really I just kept the same page open in front of me and looked through my eyelashes at Danny.

I watched his hands, watched him hold a glass—the smooth curve of it against his palm. I watched him lean over to get a bottle from under the bar, watched the muscles of his back sliding against his shirt. I watched him run his hands through his hair, push it out of his eyes, and had to remind myself to close my mouth. I watched him lean against the bar, rest his weight against the smooth brown oak, and I envied the very wood itself. I watched him take a drink from a glass of water and saw how then his upper lip was damp and how he rubbed it on the back of his hand. I couldn't stop looking at his upper lip.

I sat at the café and surreptitiously watched him, watched the light shift through the ragged strands of his honey hair. My chest tightened, and I found it hard to breathe. I closed the book and went up to sit at the bar.

"At last!" Danny said, smiling. "You've been studying on that book *all* afternoon. What in heaven's name is it about?"

"Sugar," I said, "I haven't got the faintest idea."

Jake came around the Cave now almost as much as Danny, sitting at the bar during my slow shifts, sipping on a Natty BoHo and making laconic conversation. Sometimes when I was busy with someone else, I would catch him out of the corner of my eye studying me in a considering sort of way and then looking away and not saying anything. There was enough light, if you sat directly under one of the red bulbs, to read by, and sometimes he sat there lost in his coverless copy of Plato's *Dialogues* for a while in the early evening, before the bar got crowded. He and I talked about mythology and madness and poetry. Once we talked about W. H. Auden ("Lay your sleeping head, my love, Human on my faithless arms") and then felt very friendly toward each other after that.

"So how did you come to be sitting here reading poetry in a bar?" I asked him.

"Oh, there was this girl I knew once in Asheville."

"Lover of literature?"

"In a way. We had a slight disagreement once, and she heaved this big anthology right at my head. That sucker would have knocked me cold."

"But she missed?"

"Thank God she was drunk."

"And you kept the book?"

"I felt it was in my best interest to disarm her."

"What were you fighting about?"

"Oh, I can't remember now—I guess the same thing everybody always fights about. Either too much love or not enough. My faithless arms, in all probability. We split up as soon as she got sober."

"Well, at least you got some good reading out of it."

"I consider it a good trade, all in all. At least poetry never tries to break my head. My heart, maybe—but not my head."

That was the summer I decided to grow a garden. My happiness, like Demeter's, had taken a horticultural turn. The joke back home was that the only vegetable anybody around there was interested in was corn—and only then in liquid form. Putting in a garden in the red clay out back behind my little rented house meant that I lived there now, in this new town. It meant that I had gotten out of the hills.

I bought the seeds and baby vegetable plants at a nursery out on the highway toward Millboro. Danny and I drove out together one morning, and I felt very maternal picking out tiny baby tomato plants and strawberry plants and eggplants. We even bought a few exotic things—broccoli romanesco and artichokes, purple passion asparagus. In my mind's eye, I saw green leafy rows stretching to the horizon. I imagined Danny and me nursing our tiny plants together in the bright summer sunshine.

I did not share this particular fantasy with Danny but kept it quietly to myself—a secret vision of domesticity with him, the least domestic of guys.

The biggest problem you generally face in the warm, wet, fecund climate of the South—when it comes to vegetation, at least—is beating back the rampant growth. A lazy homeowner who neglects a friendly kudzu vine can easily, for example, wake up one morning not only unable to find his lawn ornaments but unable to get out the door of his house to look for them. It is an encouraging climate for beginning gardeners. I once saw a zucchini at the county fair that was bigger than the little girl who grew it. If a six-year-old can grow a fifty-pound zucchini, how hard can it be?

The first plants to die were the exotic ones. Some just wilted and faded away, some got eaten up by bugs, some were just *gone*, shorn off clean to the ground, when I woke up in the morning. The tomato plants were doing well, and I figured that broccoli romanesco was probably beyond me anyway, so I went back to the nursery and bought more baby tomato plants to fill the empty spaces. You can never have too many fresh-from-the-garden tomatoes.

The strawberries died next. I think they got *too* wet. Or maybe they were too dry. It's hard to know. In any case, the leaves all turned brown and dropped off. Danny stood at the edge of my battered garden plot and shook his head and looked sorrowful. Pretty soon, he started refusing to come back with me to the garden store—he felt implicated, like being an accessory to murder. "It's not that I mind gardening," he said, "but I put my foot down at wanton killing. A man has got to draw the line somewhere."

I replaced the strawberry plants with tomatoes. The tomatoes were flourishing.

The gourds withered up, the zucchini turned black, even the eggplants developed spots on their leaves and then returned to the dust. With every death, I put in a new baby tomato plant. It was a ravishing sight—more than forty tomato plants, green and leafy, reaching toward the sun, growing heavy under the weight of the little green tomatoes. You can never have too many tomatoes.

My next-door neighbor, Orla, kept a sharp eye on me from across the fence and felt justified—even obligated—to correct me in my errors.

"You're doing that wrong," she blatted out one late morning while I was watering the only pea plant, with its single precious pea pod, that had survived. Orla was a transplant from the Midwest and spoke with a flat, nasal accent of certitude. Her face looked like a snapping turtle.

"First of all," she said, taking my bewildered silence as an invitation to instruct me, "those tomato plants all need to be dusted with Sevin powder to keep off the bugs."

"It's an organic garden," I said.

"Second of all," she went on, after a brief pause of dismissal, "this isn't even the right kind of dirt for a garden. Have you had a soil test done? The whole thing will have to be plowed under and new soil dug in, and you'll have to start all over again."

She pronounced this, as she did everything, as an accepted fact, and I felt a brief wave of shame on account of my inadequate soil. It had seemed perfectly fine to me—very dirty—and I was embarrassed that I had failed to scrutinize it properly. It occurred to me after a minute, as a counterexample, that the tomatoes were flourishing, and I started to say so, but Orla had already gone on to her third point, which was basically that it was silly to grow a garden at all when the grocery store had plenty of vegetables of every type, and that frozen vegetables had just as much nutrition as fresh ones, and that although some people thought canned vegetables were less nutritious, that was not true, and you were going to add salt to them when you cooked them anyway, and everything tastes pretty much the same out of the microwave, which is much less trouble, and if you melt Velveeta on it, even men will eat it, which just goes to prove (coming around to the end with a triumphal gleam in her reptilian eye) that it was foolish to grow a garden in the first place.

I had no way of telling her that my need for a garden had nothing to do with nutrition or convenience, and that I didn't even own a microwave. I searched around in my head for words to tell her what I wanted, how much I loved my tangled jungle of vines and aphids and hopefulness and even despair, but her jaw seemed clamped down so tightly on the idea of my utter failure that, facing her certainty, I was suddenly unsure even of my own longings. In that moment, I could see how my little unkempt garden looked through her eyes, and I knew very well that she would never see it through mine.

"Oh," I said.

Orla's own yard was a smooth and uniform carpet of lawn, unbroken by so much as an azalea bush, kept in positively military discipline by Orla's husband, Lem, a middle manager at a Bible distribution wholesaler out on the highway.

"Lem has some powder in the garage that he uses to kill things," Orla said in a way that I don't think was meant to be menacing. "He'll bring you a cup of it when he gets home from work." She liked to be helpful to me, especially when I was doing things wrong.

"It's an organic garden," I said again, sort of feebly.

She dismissed that with a wave of her hand. "You wash the food before you eat it, don't you?"

As she turned away, she said over her shoulder, "You'll never grow a thing if you don't do it right," and disappeared inside her house, leaving me standing surrounded by one pea pod and a sea of tomatoes. I felt protective of them, like a mother with rowdy children, the beauty of whom no one else can see.

In the late afternoons when the shadows were long and the air had turned blue, Danny would wake up and stretch and light a cigarette, sitting up naked in bed, running one hand through his hair until it stood up all on end. I would leave him rummaging around for coffee in the kitchen and go out back to water the tomato plants. When the coffee was ready, he would bring me out a cup and then sit on the beat-up lawn chair and watch me and we would talk.

"Why did you come to Waterville?" he asked me once.

"No special reason. It was a town I had heard of and that the bus went to. My uncle Joe thought that maybe someday I might be able to go to the college, or at least sign up for some courses or something. He wants that for me. I didn't really mind too much where it was that I went."

"Just somewhere else?"

"Just somewhere new."

Despite apparently having done everything wrong, by August I was drowning in my sea of tomatoes, going under like the band leader on the *Titanic*. I gave a dozen tomatoes to Orla, who accepted them but told me that store-bought were just as good. I brought some to Commie Tom, who praised their valiant redness and ate them like apples, sitting with Rosalita on the porch of the bookstore. Vera and Rafi and Pancho all took some home with them. I took a bag of ripe tomatoes to Blossom every afternoon until finally she became suspicious.

"How many tomato plants do you have?" she asked.

"Forty-seven," I said.

"Oh, honey," she said, and patted my hand, "you're going to need help."

"I tell her that," Danny said, not very paternally. "*Professional* help."

"You hush," Blossom said to him. And then to me: "I'll be at your house tomorrow after the breakfast rush is done. Do you have any canning jars?"

So Blossom and I canned tomatoes all the next day and the day after that.

In the mornings, my kitchen was green and cool, a quivering liquid light filtering through the leaves outside the windows. At night, it was yellow and still, a soft oasis of warmth with moths fluttering against the screen door. But in the August afternoons when Blossom and I slopped around in it, streaming with sweat over the boiling kettle of tomatoes, it was vivid red and far too small, hotter than outside even when outside was an oven. We propped a fan on a chair and pointed it right at us, but it didn't matter. There were dishtowels in the corners that we had used to wipe our sweaty faces until the towels were too wet, and then we dropped them on the floor and used them with our feet to mop up splashed tomato juice and spilled spices. Danny went down to the corner gas station for us and brought back grape popsicles. We ate them sitting in the living room because they melted too fast in the kitchen.

After we canned all the ripe tomatoes, we pickled the green ones in a preemptive strike designed to hold the plants' promiscuous fertility at bay at least until we recovered from the first wave.

"It won't seem so much in September," Blossom said, but Danny looked skeptical.

The jars of tomatoes were beautiful, gleaming in shiny rows on the kitchen table. We finished the last batch of pickles late the second night, and Danny and I went to bed, taking the fan with us into the bedroom. Danny felt only hot, but I felt both hot and content. I felt I had made something worth making.

Blossom took some of the jars with her, and for a long while after that, special customers got a little dish of green tomato pickles on their table at lunch. We had to do it all over again two more times before we were done. But my garden was a strange success—my dirt had redeemed itself and me somehow. Orla avoided talking to me for a whole month until an unaccountable early frost put an end to it all. She seemed to feel that I had brought the frost on myself through moral laxity and all but told me so. It made her more cheerful.

Charlie Blue washed dishes at Tia's and played pool on his nights off in the back room of the Cave. It was a hot night. The back door was propped open with a box fan sitting in it to try to get the air circulating, but my bare legs still felt sticky against the plastic chair I was sitting on to watch him. He was playing pool for money—a dollar a game—which a sign tacked up on the wall said was against the rules. He was beating the wait staff from the Fiddlehead Fern one game after another. We barely knew each other then, but he brushed his hand on my shoulder when he walked past me. I brought him back a new beer when I went up front to get one for myself. He held the cold bottle for a minute against his face. Then he lit two cigarettes at once and gave me one without my asking.

"Thanks, man," I heard Danny say.

He had materialized silently behind me, coming in from the front room. He took a drag off the cigarette and then handed it back to me. Charlie Blue just grinned and shrugged and turned back to his game. Danny pulled up another chair next to mine and put his hand on the back of my neck.

"It sure is hot back here," he said slowly, looking at me with one eyebrow up.

"Well, I guess it's starting to cool off now."

"That's good."

"Yes," I said after a pause. "You know, up to a point, though. I mean, no one wants it exactly to be winter now. No one wants it to be too cold. A person likes to know what season it is, after all."

I looked at him out of the corner of my eye.

"I'll tell you what, sugar," he said, slowly running his hand down my back. "If you start to get too cold, you just let me know and I'll figure out a way to change the weather."

What is it like for the chosen prisoner to leave the cave?

Plato says that at first the prisoner, having been freed from his chains and compelled to stand and turn around, would be dazzled and confused by the sights before him. The apparatus of his world—the fire, the carriers on the path, the figures of stone and wood—would be revealed to him. And he would be told by the gods that all the things he loved before were only shadows.

He would be told by those who know the truth that everything he knew before was lies. He is dragged forward, away.

But the prisoner, in his confusion and his fear, Socrates tells Glaucon, would obstinately resist. He wants to go back to his place with the other prisoners in the sultry atmosphere of the cave, in the world he and his fellows made together out of shadows and echoes and stories told to each other over the years. Imagine his relief when he finds his old spot. Imagine the tenderness with which he regards his forsaken shackles.

But eventually, the chosen prisoner is compelled by his captors to leave his place beside the others, to begin his journey toward the mouth of the cave.

How hard it must be to leave the warmth of the great fire and the conviviality of the other prisoners. How hard it must be to go off on one's own without them, without the others who have always been with you.

Does the prisoner have a guide—one of the cave gods—to take him by the hand, to lead him with words of comfort and assurance along the way? Or does he go alone, groping in the darkness toward the distant glimmering that is the entrance to the cave? Does it matter? Could a companion ever do anything more than watch over the prisoner, hoping for the best but knowing that the journey to the light is always—by necessity— a journey taken in solitude?

And what of the companion—the one whose role it might be to watch over the traveler? He is there to care for the traveler; that is his only purpose. What does he feel as he oversees the progress, halting and unsure, of his charge? Even at the very beginning of the journey, the companion knows what is waiting at the end. He is proud and heartbroken.

The United States entered the first Gulf War at the end of the summer. During the late afternoons down in the Cave, the radio preachers were preempted by news reports, and we sat glum and silent, listening. Tom put up a big hand-lettered sign that said, "No Blood For Oil!" in the bookstore window next to Che and came back the next morning to find a brick in the Gandhi section and shattered window glass all over the front of the store.

When there weren't customers in the bookstore who needed help, Rosalita mostly sat curled up at the far end of the couch, reading the stock. Every now and then, something would occur to her, and she would look up from her book and wait for Tom to see her looking at him.

"*Cariño mio, ¿por qué no tenemos las historias de Oriente Medio en español?*"

"Ah, what a good idea! Is there an especially good one?"

"*No lo sé.*"

"I'll find out—will you help me find out?"

"*Si, querida.*"

And she would go back to her book.

So Tom ordered a dozen different books in Spanish on Middle Eastern politics and history, as well as a big compendium of Arabic love poetry that never made it out to the shelves.

"Do you and Tom ever talk about anything other than politics?" I asked Rosalita.

"Oh, yes!" she said, but she did not tell me what.

Hank was a Vietnam vet and began wearing an olive-drab jacket with lots of insignia all over it, even in the heat of the day, to show his support for the new American war. Stinky had spent the Vietnam era getting stoned at home on account of working for eight and a half years on a Ph.D. from a school he found advertised in the back of *Rolling Stone*, but he nevertheless visited an army surplus store in Millboro and got himself a jacket even more festooned than Hank's. He also started looking sideways at Rafi and muttering things we could never quite catch.

"What's that you say there, Stinky?" Vera finally asked him.

Stinky looked startled for a second and then turned around on his barstool with his back toward Vera.

"Nothing to concern you," he muttered. "Just cogitating to myself."

"Because I thought maybe," Vera said, moving back into Stinky's line of sight, "that you seem to have a problem with one of my bartenders."

Stinky was picking at the label on his beer bottle and wouldn't meet Vera's eye. Even in the dim light, I could see a red flush starting on his neck and rising.

"Vera, how about when I have something to say, I will apprise you of that fact?"

"Look, Stinky, either say it or don't say it."

Stinky darted a look at Hank, but Hank was very carefully drinking his beer.

"Why, Vera." Here Stinky gave a quick, hollow laugh. "I mean, Rafi here, no offense"—darting his eyes over to Rafi— "he's a Moslem, right?"

"Coptic Christian, actually," Rafi volunteered.

"Same difference," Stinky said.

"Probably," Rafi shrugged.

"I think you're getting yourselves beside the point here," Stinky said with an exaggerated sigh.

"Well, tell us, Stinky," Vera said. "Just what is your point?"

"The *point*," Stinky said, "is that the founding fathers of this country did not come here all the way from Britain just to see the place overrun with a bunch of foreigners." To Rafi: "No offense."

"None taken," Rafi said.

"Do you ever listen to yourself?" Vera asked him.

"Don't deny it, Vera. The very foundation of this nation is that this country is for Americans only. That is what we fought the American Revolution for."

"And now Iraq is for Americans only, too?"

"Don't be purposefully obtuse. We are bringing American-style freedom to people who are basically, for all intents and purposes, barbarians. I mean, those people over there have no respect for life, no respect for the sovereign rights of others, no respect for basic human dignity and freedom and the Constitution of the United States. For all intents and purposes, they're animals. No offense."

"None taken," Rafi said.

"This war is to bring enlightenment values to people who are savages."

"I thought it was for oil."

"Good grief! We couldn't continue to have this great nation, this shining beacon of civilization, if we didn't utilize oil to run it, could we? You have got to think these things through!"

"I'm starting to get a headache," Vera said.

"Now the issue at hand here," Stinky continued, "is that the Moslem-persuasion people—no offense—should not be on American soil. They need to be back in their own country."

"So they can be civilized into American values?"

"Yes! That's right! Finally you are starting to be elucidated by my point!"

"Stinky," Vera said, "you are an idiot."

"No offense," Rafi said.

I laughed, and so did Vera. Hank had a mouthful of beer, and it squirted out his nose. Stinky turned bright red.

"I don't have to sit here and take this," he said. "I don't have to be insulted by the likes of you. Stay ignorant—it makes no matter to me." He got up from his barstool.

"And another thing—I'm not paying for that beer!" Stinky spat, and then hurried out and up the stairs.

The war had a momentum of its own now. It dominated the kitchen-table talk at Boystown. Tom got up several petitions and a pretty good-sized march down Juniper Street. Rafi got shouted at two different times by people who took exception to his skin color, and Jordan was taunted by a cherub-faced child in his preschool class. Orla and Lem hung an enormous American flag from the gutter on the front of their house, but Orla and I did not discuss the war, restricting our conversations as always to my horticultural ineptitude and loose morals.

I listened to the news reports, of course, and talked about them with everyone else and marched with Tom and wrote my congressman. But it still seemed so far away—I didn't see then that it could ever really touch me. Late at night in the Cave, Pancho still played Beethoven, and even later, Danny and I lay side by side in bed with the windows open and the night sounds lulling us to sleep.

The soul, Socrates says, is like a charioteer driving a chariot with two winged horses. One of the horses is good and pure and pulls the chariot upward on strong wings until at last, from a place even above heaven, the charioteer has a perfect view of Justice, Knowledge, and Beauty. In this place above heaven, there are serene green pastures where the winged horse will be fed.

But the chariot has two horses, and while one is noble, pulling for the pastures above the sky, the other is fractious and ungovernable, a wild thing fighting against his brother, eager to go his own way and escape his harness. Rather than rising steadily toward heaven, the unruly horse wrestles the chariot into Chaos. The two horses of our soul struggle against each other so that the chariot's progress is uncertain and haphazard. Sometimes the pure horse briefly prevails and the charioteer glimpses the perfections of the realm above heaven. But the glimpse is always fleeting because the wild and unruly horse can never be fully conquered, and the struggle between the two is always renewed.

Socrates does not say so directly, but it seems that the unruly horse is the stronger of the two. Human souls do not inhabit, as a rule, the pastures of serenity. Instead, for the most part, our souls struggle and flail in the chaotic world below.

But some souls, though residing in the darkness that is mortal life, nevertheless remember the glimpse they have had of Justice, Knowledge, and Beauty. Even in the midst of earthbound mortality, they are on the lookout again for the realm above eaven. These are the people who have visions, the people who have dreams.

Socrates says we call them "mad"—those whose souls have not forgotten the glimpse of a place beyond heaven, those who keep their eyes focused there, on the fields that other mortals can't see or have forgotten. They are called mad, but Socrates argues that instead they should be called "lovers."

Love, he says, is the proper response to the sight of Justice,

Knowledge, and Beauty. Those who have seen beyond this world yearn to return to the place above heaven, and only in the pure and selfless devotion of the lover can we regain it. The purity of our Love suffuses our gaze, and the light of our yearning for heaven illuminates the things we see on earth. In our beloved, we see again the perfection of the realm above. The vision of the realm calls to our souls, rekindling our memories, overpowering us with longing to be once more in the green pastures of forever. Enthralled by our vision, we are helpless to look away.

Love and madness, Socrates says, are twin gifts of our soul. They are the price we pay for the memory of heaven. Our insatiable yearning is all we have left of paradise.

In the woods west of Millboro was a spring-fed pond surrounded by pine trees and quiet. It was probably on someone's private property, but I never knew whose. We called it "Lost Pond" and went there—sometimes just Danny and me alone and sometimes with other people, Rafi and Billy Joe or Jake—on deep moonlit nights when we weren't working or just before sunrise on nights when we were. Tom came with Rosalita once or twice, and by then we could tell that a baby was on the way.

The water was warm and inclined to be somewhat weedy except over the cold springs that fed the pond, where it was suddenly cool and deep and clear. There was a rough plank boat dock that dipped and swayed at the edge of the water, and we would sit on it, pulling our shivering knees together, Danny with his arms around me. We would drink vodka from a bottle that we kept bobbing on the surface of the water next to us. We shivered, I think, more from the beauty of the night than from the temperature of it—we were never really cold enough to need the blanket we brought with us.

Maybe it was the beauty or maybe it was the vodka that went to Danny's head. Whatever the case, it wasn't too long after we'd finished canning the tomatoes that he pulled me close to him one night alone at the dock and, whispering into my mouth, asked me if I loved him. In such a situation, there is no answer other than yes.

Even at nighttime, it is possible to fly right up to the very edge of the sun.

AUTUMN

IT USED TO BE THAT IF YOU drove south from town, heading toward Millboro, first you passed Honeysuckle Road and then, a mile or so later, Dandelion Road and then nothing for a long time until you crossed Wildwood Drive. That was the last paved crossroad. After that, you started counting mailboxes. The mailboxes stood in rickety little congregations huddled together by the side of the asphalt so that people who lived scattered out in the woods had to come up to the road to get their mail. At the seventh cluster of mailboxes after Wildwood Drive, there was a gap in the trees and a dirt trail, just wide enough for a narrow car, that led off down to the right. The trail split at a big tree stump. The left-hand fork wound through more woods and then a meadow where we used to see foxes and then ended at a three-room cabin with a brook behind it and woods of pine and dogwood all around it. There was a fireplace and a tiny wooden deck perched above the brook where we thought we would make love all the time. Danny and I went to live there together when my lease was up at the end of September.

If you are in love, pokey little cabins in the woods seem magic and beautiful and you don't notice things like the way the whole place smells like mold or how the lights work only intermittently or how spiders are always in the bathtub. Or, if you do notice those things, it is only because they seem funny and endearing, and you make jokes about them together and eat dinner by candlelight together and fight off the spiders together. If you are in love, any dump seems like heaven, and really it is. When we die and finally reach the afterlife, I don't guess we will care at all about the furnishings—we will care only that the people we love are there.

Our friends all came by the first evening after we moved in and brought housewarming gifts and drank wine and tequila and beer with us. Tom and Rosalita brought us a copy of Friedrich Engels's *The Origin of the Family, Private Property and the State* that still had the cover on. Vera brought us a case of Dutch beer in bottles. Billy Joe made us a bedside table, and Rafi painted it to look like a cow. Pancho made us a cassette tape of Beethoven piano sonatas, and Blossom brought a sweet potato pie, a cherry pie, a black-bottom rum pie, and a whole salt-cured ham. Jake brought us *The Collected Poems of W. H. Auden*, but he never actually gave it to us—just left it on the kitchen table and then went home.

Everybody else stayed all night, and we ran around in the woods and howled at the moon. Just at dawn, Pancho and Pamela decided to sing hymns about the Jordan River down by the tiny stream, and their voices echoed together among the trees like skylarks. Danny said he thought he saw them kiss, but nothing came of it then, and Danny eventually admitted he wasn't really sure after all.

Before I moved, Orla had come over and sat on the third-hand couch in my living room, watching me as I packed boxes.

"You certainly weren't here very long," she said.

"Well, I only had a six-month lease."

"You could have renewed it, I'm sure."

"Um, well, a friend of mine found a place out toward Millboro that we're going to share. It'll be a lot cheaper."

"A friend?"

Orla had spied Danny coming home with me at dawn or kissing me goodbye in the doorway in the afternoon or sacked out all day under the shade trees out back, but she had never spoken to him.

"A friend," I said, wrapping newspaper around some mismatched dishes. "My boyfriend."

Orla pursed her lips. "A boyfriend," she said skeptically. "Someone you've known quite awhile, I guess?"

"Awhile," I said evasively.

"Girls these days move so *fast*," she said.

"Well, there's a war on, you know."

Orla just looked blankly at me.

"Girls these days don't set much store by marriage anymore, I guess," she sighed after a minute, and shook her head in a pitying way.

"We'll get married," I said too quickly.

Orla shook her head again. "Girls always think so, I'm sure," she said.

There was wild honking outside as Danny and Billy Joe pulled up in Billy Joe's truck to get the furniture.

"They're here," I said to Orla. "We're going to need that couch now."

"Girls always think so," she said again, getting up.

She left by the back door without meeting Danny.

Jake and I were alone in the bar. He was drinking his first Natty BoHo, and I was leaning on the cash register, watching *Jeopardy!* with the sound off. I was telling him about my conversation with Orla.

"Do you want to be married?" he asked me.

"To Danny?" I said.

"No—just to anyone. Do you want that?"

"Well, we're supposed to want it, right? Aren't we all supposed to want to find true love—forever?"

"Do you know anyone who is married and who is happy?"

I thought about it for a minute.

"No," I said. "But then again, I don't know anyone who is unmarried who is happy either."

"Aren't you happy?"

"I'm happy with Danny."

"It's not the same thing, is it?"

"Besides, he hasn't asked me to marry him. That was just something I said to my neighbor to get her to shut up. He's never brought up marriage at all."

"He will."

"How do you know?"

"Because he always does—he can't help himself. Danny is a romantic."

"Liar," I said. "Who has he asked to marry him?"

"You can't believe he doesn't have a past—that you're the only one he's ever loved."

"Of course not," I said, a sinking feeling in my stomach. "But I'm the one he loves now." I remembered again how I had never liked Jake. "What do you care about it anyway?"

"I don't care, actually," Jake said. "Just making conversation."

He turned back to his beer, and I turned the volume up on the television. I wished he would go away, but he just stayed there watching the end of *Jeopardy!* and then reruns of *Gilligan's Island* and *The Addams Family*. He was still there, very drunk but quiet, when Rafi came in to relieve me at eight. I went straight home, but Danny was out, so I ate a sandwich from the last of Blossom's ham and went to bed.

♦♦♦

When I told Jake that I wasn't thinking about marriage, I was lying. Because once I had said the word to Orla, it became stuck in my head, stubborn and sulking, like a brooding unsociable guest who hates the party but nevertheless doesn't leave. Marriage to Danny—the idea of it colored the afternoon silence after we made love, lurked in the corners of our little cabin in the woods, watched us at the grocery store while we bought bread and eggs and in the bar where other boys never flirted with me anymore and where the seat next to him was always for me. I never said the word out loud to Danny, but he heard it anyway.

He went without me every week to visit his parents where they lived out in the country on the other side of Millboro. While he was gone, I washed dishes or cleaned the bathtub or watched TV or went down to the Cave and got drunk.

"Do your parents know I exist?" I asked him.

"Exist in what way?" he said.

"What do you mean 'in what way'? How many ways are there?"

"Do you mean do they know I have a girlfriend, or do you mean they know it's you and who you are and all about you, or what?"

"Do they know you live here with me?"

"They know I'm sharing a house with you. They haven't inquired into the sleeping arrangements too closely."

"Do they know my name?"

"Believe me, sugar, you don't want to do this."

"Do what?"

"You don't want to get mixed up with all that—with my family. You don't want them coming in here and making themselves part of our life. We're happy now just like this, aren't we? Let's leave it be."

So I didn't say any more, didn't mention it that night or all the next day. But I didn't stop thinking about it.

Finally, late the second day, Danny broke.

"Okay, okay, okay!" he said out of the blue. "I give up! I'll take you to meet them."

"I'm sure it will be nice," I said.

"Just don't say I didn't warn you."

Danny took me to meet his parents on a warm Sunday afternoon. Late-autumn katydids were buzzing from the high grass as we rolled by, Danny driving and me watching his profile silhouetted in the dizzy bright sunshine from the car window. We drove south from our house, heading toward Millboro and then through it, passing the roadside filigree of tiny cornfields, gray wooden houses, little strips of gas stations and grocery stores, patches of pine forest, and scrap yards of rusting pickup trucks that decorated the edges of Old U.S. 213, mostly forgotten now that the new 213 had been built. We had the windows down.

The brick house Danny's parents had built with the insurance money (after the wooden house he had grown up in burned to the ground in a suspicious incident involving cheap tequila and Danny on the roof installing an electric attic fan) sat close to the road with a new butter yellow Cadillac parked in the gravel under the carport at the side of the house and a faux-stained-glass ornament hanging in the front window that spelled out in Gothic lettering, "This HOME Protected By JESUS." It featured a disembodied, presumably heavenly, and somewhat glowering pair of eyes that seemed to be sending out sizzling beams of yellow light on to the letters below them. Underneath that, in the very bottom corner of the window, was a sticker that said, "Protected by ADT Security Systems." A sort of trust-but-verify attitude toward heavenly intervention that probably should have been comforting. I saw the two crocheted cats propped up in a side window and realized suddenly that I was out of my league.

We entered through the side door, straight into the kitchen. Danny didn't knock; he had let go of my hand. His parents were sitting together at the kitchen table, drinking coffee, but he called out, "Anybody home?" anyway. The kitchen smelled delicately of air freshener.

Danny's parents had had him late in life—*old* was the word he used for them more than any other. And they *were* old—with thin, papery skin that dissolved into relief maps of wrinkles like aerial photographs of drought-stricken lake beds, wispy white hair almost gone from his dad's head and curled into pristine rigidity on his mom's.

For a couple of such radically old and withered-type people, his parents had not lost the capacity for the strip-you-bare appraising glance. His mom did an amazing imitation of the Jesus eyes in the front window, lacking only the death rays of yellow light, and turned her whole body toward me.

"Now let's see here, where are you from?" she asked in a lipless drawl. "Your *people*, I mean."

My *people*. I remembered my mother, one long-ago morning,

gently brushing Belle's silky hair and tying a blue ribbon in it and then, catching sight of me lurking in the doorway, turning away as if she hadn't seen me. I thought of Uncle Joe letting out a whoop the first time I hit one of the cans balanced on the top rail of the fence. My *people*.

I tried to subdue my uncouth backwoods twang and dial up my best genteel Deep South accent. After an entire adolescence of repeatedly watching *Gone With the Wind* on the cable channel out of Atlanta, I felt that anything was possible. I took a shot at Scarlett O'Hara but in the pressure of the moment missed and got Prissy instead. I babbled a bit while his mom stared at me and pursed her lips (which did nothing for my ability to form a coherent sentence), and I began to understand more viscerally what Danny had been doing on the roof with cheap tequila in the first place.

"Yes," his mom said finally, a long, sibilant syllable that very obviously meant *no*.

His dad turned to Danny. "Y'all should have come down earlier, Daniel. Reverend Tucker asked after you at church, wondering how you're doing. You know he always asks after you."

"We knew another Catholic girl once," his mom interjected to me faux-conversationally, making it clear that I had been discussed more thoroughly than Danny let on. "You remember that red-headed Barnett girl in your senior class, Daniel, whose daddy was in the highway management? They were foreigners."

"They were from Virginia," Danny said with a little sigh that meant this was not a whole new fresh conversation we were having here.

"She became a nun."

"A nun?" Danny said. This was apparently news to him.

"She had to go to Charlotte to do it," his mother smiled at me.

"Now, after the war," his dad said to me, "I used to go down to Charlotte just about every month. Because of the fire department." Danny's father had been instrumental in setting up the local volunteer fire department, which of course made the whole attic fan/cheap tequila incident all the more ironic.

"Oh?" I said, trying to be polite. "What did the fire department need to do in Charlotte?"

His mom looked at me incredulously. "They needed to put out fires," she said.

"But Charlotte's miles and miles from here," I started.

"Well, honey, they have fires miles from here, too. There's fires all over," his mom said with a small, ambiguous chuckle.

"Do they still have that Lunch Box Diner on Trade Street there?" his dad asked me. "What's the cross street? It's near the hardware store."

"I've never been to Charlotte," I said.

"You haven't even visited it?" He sounded very surprised at this.

"Daniel," his mom began, "Arnold was at church this morning. He said to tell you hello. He's in the bank now. His daddy took him on last spring."

"I would at least visit it first, if it was me," his dad admonished me. "I know the bus goes down there because after the war we used to take it for the fire department. We took it from Waterville."

"That sounds nice," I mumbled, confused. I felt that one or the other of us was not tracking properly on this conversation.

"And of course, Robin was there. She's such a nice girl," said his mom, eyeing my boots.

"The corner of Trade and Graham!" his dad crowed with delight. "Next to the hardware store." Then his face fell into a frown of doubt. "I don't suppose," he said to me, "that you'll get out to eat much."

"She always asks after you," Danny's mother continued. "You really should go by sometime and see her. I know she'd be so tickled to see you anytime." She turned to me. "I'm sure Daniel has told you all about Robin, of course."

"Well, I guess we'd better be going," Danny said.

"Why, no, he hasn't," I said.

"It's a long drive back," Danny said.

"Gracious!" His mom definitely chuckled now. "They were inseparable, just inseparable!"

"Of course," his dad added thoughtfully, "no one knows what you look like under there, so you might as well eat what you want."

"High school was a long time ago, Mama," Danny said.

"Might as well get whatever pleasures you can," said his dad.

"Not to look at Robin, it wasn't," countered his mom. "Her figure looks just as slim and pretty as it did the day y'all graduated."

"Is gluttony still a sin for y'all?" his dad asked me, looking concerned and holding up his fingers to count off. "There's pride, I know, and fornication . . . ."

"We really have to go now," Danny said, standing up and heading to the door.

"Good luck in Charlotte!" his dad called.

"Is there any particular reason why your dad thinks I'm going to become a nun in Charlotte?" I asked Danny once we hit the highway.

"Not that I know of," Danny said, and then laughed. "I tried to warn you. Now let's go home and figure out a way to forget them, okay?"

Summer lingered for a long time that year, but eventually the sky turned a hard steel color and the dogwoods dropped their leaves and the crows began to sound mournful calling to each other from the edges of the meadow, which is how you know that it is autumn at last.

Danny and I found a not-too-bad love seat at the dump and put it in front of our empty, ash-scattered fireplace and fully intended to spend our evenings cuddling before a roaring blaze. Danny went so far as to borrow a firewood ax from his cousin and to lean it up against the side of the house.

We had no neighbors out in the woods and easily could have spent all day fornicating on the deck—or in the middle of the road, for that matter—without being disturbed by anyone. But the weather had turned raw and gritty and inhospitable to exposed skin. The fallen dead leaves were slippery and damp, clinging like slugs to the outdoor furniture so you were never quite sure what you were feeling when you accidently touched one. Inside the house, the light was a perpetual gloom and we kept the lamps lit all day long. Danny was gone most nights until late.

Charlie Blue and I were sitting down at the end of the bar when Tom came in after closing up the bookstore and asked Rafi for a Natty BoHo.

"When did you learn to play bass so well?" Tom asked Charlie.

Charlie blushed and smiled and looked down at his beer. "Oh, I've just been picking at it some," he said. "Just, you know, to kind of pass the time. I don't really know how to play much."

"Why don't you start playing out more?" Tom asked him. "You could get together some folks to play with, I bet."

Charlie blushed some more and didn't take his eyes off his beer. "Oh, I just play from time to time," he said. "Just kind of on the spur of the moment. I couldn't go onto a stage or anything like that."

"You did here."

"Well, it's different here. I mean, it's just us here, you know. Friends . . . "

"I'd go see you play," said Tom.

"We all would," Rafi said, looking down the bar.

"Not me," said Stinky, who had been shouting out a string of wrong answers to *Jeopardy!* and was looking disgusted with the TV.

"See?" Rafi said. "It would be perfect."

Charlie grinned down into his beer.

"The problem in this town," Stinky said, ignoring Rafi, "is that every two-bit circus pony thinks he's the horse of the year. Some things are best left to be effectuated by the professionals. Who wants to listen to amateur hour? I mean, as a musician, you're not exactly that hula hoop guy."

There was a pause while we all thought about it.

"Yo-Yo Ma?" Tom said.

Stinky gave Tom a withering stare and pointedly turned back to *Jeopardy!* "Morons," he muttered under his breath.

"Ignore him," I said.

"He's got a point, though," Charlie said. "I'm no professional musician. I'm no Billy Joe."

"Let me tell you," Rafi said. "I've known Billy Joe for almost a thousand years now, and even Billy Joe didn't used to be Billy Joe."

"Who'd he used to be?" Charlie asked.

Stinky snorted with his back to us.

"Just another kid with a secondhand guitar," Rafi said.

"Still is," Stinky said to the room.

"Maybe in some ways he still is," Tom said. "But that's the beauty of it."

"How do you mean?" Charlie said.

"I mean that we're all in it together—just human animals here on earth together for a short time. If we can make some music and share it with each other, well, then I guess we've done some good in the world."

"Oh, brother," Stinky said to the TV screen.

"I'll tell you what," Rafi said to Charlie. "Billy Joe is at the house right now, and I bet he's not doing anything much. Why don't you go on over there and bring your bass and play some with him for a little bit?"

"Oh, I couldn't just barge in like that."

"Come on," Tom said. "I'll go with you. Billy Joe will be happy to see us. We'll bring beer."

Charlie looked doubtful, but he got up off his barstool. Rafi filled a brown paper bag with cold beer and handed it to him. Tom pulled out his wallet.

"No charge," Rafi said.

After they left, I said to Rafi, "Tom sure is a nice guy."

"Nothing nice about it," Stinky said, turning to look at me. "Take my word for it—it's a pretty near certitude that, statistically speaking, Charlie Blue will just end up another failure. Uneducated punk kid like that? He'll never amount to anything, future-wise. Tom's just setting him up for a fall. Nothing nice about it."

"How do you know?" I said.

"Seen it too many times, little lady," he said. "He'll end up just another loser sitting in a bar."

Stinky got up and paid his tab and left a nickel for a tip.

"You come back soon, now," Rafi said as the door closed behind Stinky.

A couple of months later, I ran into Orla for the first time since I had moved. We were both buying cardboard-tasting winter tomatoes in the produce section of the big supermarket. She was happy to see me, especially in such a compromising position. I was like a Baptist preacher being caught with two hookers and a basketful of porn.

"I didn't see your wedding announcement in the paper," she said. "I looked and looked. Didn't you put one in?"

"We're not married yet," I said.

"Hmm," Orla said.

"We're going to get married, but we just haven't yet," I said.

"Hmm," Orla said again.

"There are so many details to take care of," I said, and laughed uneasily, feeling unaccountably panicky, like when you're driving down the road, minding your own business, and you suddenly notice the car behind you is a cop. Even though you're not doing anything wrong, you start to worry.

"We're thinking of June!" I semi-shrieked.

Orla leaned forward and gently patted my oddly sweaty hand. She looked deep into my eyes with a small, sad smile. "I'll pray for you," she said. Then she patted my hand again and walked off toward the snack aisle.

It is one of the ironies of Christianity that Saturday night turns so seamlessly into Sunday morning. Danny was face down on the pillow with his arm flung out across my belly. I could feel the warmth of him and hear the quiet sound of his breathing. He was awake.

"We've got to get up now," he said. "I promised my folks that we'd come by after church and eat lunch with them."

"You what?"

"It was either that or have them here."

"Lord, anything but that."

"Do we have an iron?" he asked, sitting up.

"Like for clothes?"

"There has been some discussion of wrinkled shirts from my mother, and I thought it might be best to head that off at the pass."

We had no iron, but he found a sweater with only one smallish hole and a pair of pants that had been worn only once since they were last washed. I put on the dress Uncle Joe had bought me for my high-school graduation.

"I'll hit you if you laugh," I said to Danny.

He didn't laugh.

"It's just that they have these ideas," he said. "They have these ways that they believe things should be."

"What do they believe?" I asked.

"Well, for one thing, they believe that hell is real, and they believe that I might be going there."

"Nice parents," I said.

"It's just that they love me," he said. "They want so much for me. Better than they had it."

So we drove out on the old blacktop highway, not saying much—just watching the empty winter fields roll past. We arrived at their house and pulled up to the driveway at the same time as Danny's parents.

"Oh, Daniel, there you are," his mom said, getting out of their car under the roof of the carport. "I thought you might join us in church this morning."

"No," Danny said, looking vague. "No, we were in town."

"Must be a mighty good preacher there to hold a candle to Reverend Tucker."

"How's Charlotte?" his dad asked me as we went into the kitchen.

"Charlotte who?" I said.

"I knew a girl named Charlotte once," he said. Then he paused and smiled. "Now she most definitely was not a nun!"

"Hush, Daddy!" Danny's mom said reprovingly. "There's no call for that kind of conversation."

Danny's dad hushed, but I noticed that the smile lingered on his face for some time.

"Daniel." She turned to him. "There was a sale on out at the JCPenney and I bought you two new pairs of nice everyday slacks." She was beadily eyeing the pants we had been so happy to find that morning. "They're in your room, and you can try them on now."

"Mama," Danny began, but she cut him off with a sharp bark—"Daniel!"—and he got wearily to his feet.

"Charlotte used to wear pants sometimes," Danny's father broke in. "Young ladies didn't wear pants too often in those days, of course. I remember a certain white pair she had . . . ."

"No nonsense, now," Danny's mother said severely, possibly to both Danny and his dad, and then turned to me, smiling with obvious effort. "Boys will be such boys!" she said. "No matter how old they get, they always need a firm hand."

"Firm!" his dad said, smiling into space.

"You seem like the sort of . . . ," she paused, "young lady who knows how to . . . ," another pause, "handle menfolk."

"Well . . . ," I started, thinking that both yes and no were bad answers to this question.

But Danny's mother carried on. "Why, they're just like children, all of them! They don't know what's good for themselves, no matter how many times you tell them!"

"Be sure to tell her I said hello," Danny's dad said. He reached out and patted my hand.

"Take Daniel," Danny's mother continued.

"No, I wouldn't take Daniel along, if I were you." Danny's father shook his head and then lowered his voice to a conspiratorial whisper. "Charlotte's an awful pretty girl—you should see her in pants!" He winked.

"He has so much potential!" Danny's mother said. "That's what I always tell him. He could do things with himself, if he just showed a little gumption! Or if the right woman would settle him down. Like his cousin Bob Henry—he's just almost exactly Daniel's age, and he already runs four fried-fish sandwich franchises between here and Tennessee. Now there's no reason in the world why Daniel couldn't do that just as well. Or even better—half a dozen franchises! Why, when they were boys, Daniel could just run rings around Bob Henry."

"Is Bob Henry the one all the cats follow around?" his dad asked.

"Now Daddy, you know Bob Henry!" Then, turning to me, "I'm not saying Bob Henry couldn't maybe spend a little longer in the shower some days. It might help with his acne some, too. But that's beside the point. The point is that he's made something out of himself. You can't say running four fried-fish sandwich franchises isn't making something of yourself!"

"And cats sure do seem to like him," Danny's dad said, nodding vigorously.

"If he would use lye soap . . . ," Danny's mother began, but just then Danny appeared, looking resigned in a pair of khaki pants with pleats in the front. They seemed to come up especially high on his waist.

"Now don't you look nice!" Danny's mother said. "So much better than those ratty things you had on."

"Thank you, Mama," Danny said morosely.

"Kiss your mama who takes such good care of you," she said, and he trudged over and kissed her cheek.

"Now let's have lunch," she said. "You look like you could use a good home-cooked meal for a change."

We ate baked ham with macaroni salad, potato salad, cole-slaw, and three-bean salad. Danny didn't say too much, and we left as soon as we could after lunch.

On the way out, his dad leaned in close to me in the carport. "Don't forget to tell Charlotte I said hello," he whispered, and winked again.

Later that day, I asked Danny, "What was your mother like when you were little?"

He thought for a minute.

"Disappointed," he said.

"I know the feeling. I think my mama would have liked me better if only I would have been all done up in a frilly pink dress all the time. But I don't remember her ever buying me anything like that—or ribbons or shiny shoes. Those sorts of things were never for me."

"Be glad. At least you weren't paraded around in front of everyone dressed up like a prizewinning goose at Easter."

"No," I said. "I was never paraded around."

Autumn wore on and slowly turned into winter—the Southern winter that is really just a long extension of fall, gray and sad and defeated and endless. Danny and I got used to living together and gradually didn't go as much into town on cold nights to keep each other company at work. I worked mostly afternoons and then went home and watched the war on TV. Jake stopped by every now and then and drank beer and watched with me.

Sometimes Danny came home early, and we watched the war together until the TV station went off the air. Summertime seemed longer ago than it really was.

In the mornings, I would wake up and find Danny asleep close to me, one arm flung over his head, his fingers gently curved as if he were cradling a handful of air. I wouldn't touch his hand for fear of waking him, but I would very carefully lay my own hand next to his on the sheets and try to feel the warmth of his body heat.

How well I know this hand, I would tell myself, marveling at the construction of it—the way the bones and muscles fit together, the way the skin was molded so perfectly against them, the way my own hand could have been cupped so effortlessly into his palm.

My hand belongs in your hand, I would think, looking at them next to each other. *Your hand belongs with mine and we belong together and you belong to me.*

When I got out of bed to go make coffee and start my day, I was very quiet, so as not to disturb him, and sometimes he was still asleep when I left to go to work, his hand still curled into the empty air.

There weren't people down at the pond very often, now that the weather had turned. The water was too cold at night and too forlorn looking in the daytime. I went down and sat on the dock sometimes by myself when Danny wasn't around.

Pancho was there one night lying flat on his back listening to the water slap against the dock while he stared up at the star-filled sky.

"Whatcha see, Pancho?" I asked.

"Storm's coming," he said.

I looked up at the darkness. "There aren't any clouds," I said.

"There are lots of different kinds of clouds."

"Sky looks pretty clear to me."

"Yes, it looks clear," he agreed. "But I can feel a storm coming in from somewhere. It's very close to us now."

"Where is it coming from?"

"I don't know. I just feel it. Maybe it's coming from somewhere we never thought a storm could come from."

"When will it get here?"

"It's been coming a long time, but I'm afraid it will be here soon."

"Should we go back into town? Will we be okay out here?"

Pancho closed his eyes and frowned in concentration for a few minutes.

"I don't think we'll all be okay," he said finally.

So I followed him back to town, and we went together to Tia's first and then down to the Cave after Tia's closed. It rained the next day, but only a drizzle.

STORM

IT GOT DARK EARLY NOW. Even though I still mostly worked the first shift, it was as black as nighttime when I got off. There were no lights out back by the dumpster behind the Cave where I parked my car.

"Wait a minute and I'll walk you out there," Rafi said when he came to relieve me. He was pulling half a dozen Buds on tap for a sullen-looking group of men who had been shooting pool all afternoon.

"Don't be silly," I said. "I'm only going twenty feet to my car."

The alley was lovely in the dark. The door of the Cave glowed with yellow light whenever anyone opened it to go in or out, and the music from the jukebox spilled out into the quiet. The air smelled like the chilies that were roasting in the kitchen at Tia's. The noise of the cars going by on Thornapple Street was muffled so it sounded like ocean waves against a beach.

A shadow moved next to the dumpster, and I saw that Stinky was standing by my car, just looking at it.

"Oh," I said. "You startled me. What are you doing just standing out here by yourself?"

He didn't answer for a minute, but turned his eyes slowly from my car to me.

"Where's your boyfriend, Danny?" he finally said, and I could tell from the sound of his voice that, even though he hadn't been in the Cave at all that afternoon, he was already drunk. It occurred to me that he probably frequented other bars as well.

"I don't know," I said. "I imagine he's around somewhere."

"He's not around right now."

"I'm sure he's around somewhere," I said again.

"He leaves you alone a lot," Stinky said, coming closer to me.

"Well, we live together now," I said. "We don't need to spend every minute with each other."

I headed toward my car, but Stinky stepped between me and it. He was close enough now that I could smell the odor of stale beer on him.

"You females all say you want to be independent," he slurred, "and that you want your space. But what you really want is a man with you all the time, giving you attention. Giving you what he's got."

"Danny gives me plenty of attention."

Stinky reached out and put his hand on my arm. "He's not giving you attention right now."

I started to pull away, and his grip tightened. I felt a flutter of panic.

"Let go of me," I said in my most no-nonsense voice. I didn't want him to know I was scared; I thought that would make it worse.

Instead of letting go, he grabbed my other arm and squeezed harder. I felt his fingernails bite into my flesh, breaking the skin.

"Why don't you scream?" he whispered. "Maybe because you don't really want me to let go?"

I tried to think of something to say that would make him release me, but I felt frozen, not able to move or to speak or to think.

"I bet you'd look really pretty down on your knees," he said.

"Let go," I said again, and tried to yank my arm free, but he held on and pushed me backward against the car.

"You'd like it," he said. "I'd make you say that you like it."

His face was so close to mine now that I could smell the stench of his breath. I brought my knee up with a quick jerk like Uncle Joe had taught me, but he blocked it with his leg and then laughed.

"Oh, yes," he hissed. "I'd make you say you like it."

I was frozen with panic. This was nothing like the high-school boys back home, who were just hoping to get what they could get. Stinky, I knew, wanted to hurt me.

"Whatcha doin', Stinky?" It was Jake, materializing next to us in the dark from out of the Cave's door.

"Just having a little private convocation here," Stinky said, dropping my arms.

"Oh, yeah? Whatcha talking about?" Jake stepped closer to Stinky so that Stinky had to take a step back.

"Don't you know what private means?" Stinky sneered.

"I know I'll kick your ass in about two minutes," Jake said. His voice was very quiet.

Stinky didn't say anything for a minute, but then dropped his eyes from Jake's face.

"Don't flatter yourself," Stinky said to me, and ambled slowly down the steps into the back door of the Cave.

I unlocked my car.

"God, he's a creep," I said to Jake, trying to sound calm, but my voice was shaky. "Thanks for being all knight-in-shining-armor for me."

Jake didn't smile. He lit two cigarettes and gave me one. I was glad he couldn't see my face in the dark.

"Don't come out here by yourself in the dark," he said.

"It's okay," I said, trying to steady my voice. "I could have just yelled, and somebody would have heard me."

"I know," he said. "I know that. But you don't need to be out here by yourself when it gets dark so early. I don't want to have to be bothered hanging around beating up drunks for you."

"Don't worry," I said. I tried to laugh, but it came out as a cough.

"Just promise."

"I promise."

He watched me get into my car and fumble with the keys before I could get it started. He stayed in the parking lot looking after me, and I could see his silhouette against the light from the back door until I turned out on to the street. I drove a block and then pulled over and vomited into the grass by the side of the road.

Danny wasn't home when I got there. I took a long hot shower, but I could still smell Stinky.

The sixth labor of Hercules was to destroy the Stymphalian birds.

The birds were the creatures of Ares, the god of war. They had terrible razor-sharp metal claws and metal beaks and metal wings, from which they shot out their metal feathers like arrows to kill men. The bloodthirsty birds then feasted on the flesh of the dead. Flocks of them had settled on Lake Stymphalos in

Arcadia, so that even in those idyllic valleys of imagination, the servants of war were lurking.

In the end, Hercules did not destroy the Stymphalian birds, but managed only to shoot some of them and drive the rest away by frightening them with the noise of a great brass rattle given to him by Athena. Like Ares himself, the birds of war—no matter how savage—were cowards at heart. They fled Arcadia and settled on the island of Ares. They were there when Jason and the Argonauts had to stop on the island during their quest for the Golden Fleece. Again the ravenous birds shot their razor feathers at the heroes, screaming down at them from the sky. But again the heroes were able to fend off the birds by frightening them with the noisy clashing of spears on their shields. The birds scattered and fled. But they were never destroyed.

The Greeks knew that the birds of war, cruel and cowardly, still lived, waiting for their chance to feast on the flesh of the dead. They were never very far, even in Arcadia.

I developed a callus on the end of my right index finger from opening beer cans and another one down the side of the same finger from opening twist-open beer bottles. In the downtown world of bars and night cafés, these twin calluses were marks of honor.

Now sometimes on Friday or Saturday nights, I would work along with Vera when things were busy. The space behind the bar was small—only three or four feet deep—and when two bartenders were working together, they had to coordinate their movements and be always aware of one another to keep from constantly colliding. And it was inevitable that someone sitting at the far back end of the bar would be drinking beers stored in the coolers under the far front end, and vice versa. Even with my calluses of honor, I was still a novice at double-bartending and could be clumsy sometimes working around another person.

But Vera was a pro and could dance down the whole length of the bar opening beers, making change, pulling drafts, ringing up tabs, and keeping disparate conversations going with different people all along the way, with only the slightest touch on my shoulder as she slipped past behind me. When she wasn't behind the bar, Vera mostly seemed tough, but when she was working, you could see how elegant she was, how graceful. When she and Rafi worked together, it was like watching a ballet. There were nights when between the two of them they served a thousand beers.

So when I worked with Vera, I relied on her skill to keep us both from ending up black and blue. The hubbub could be intense, especially if the band was any good and the bar was crowded. And yet even in the midst of all the commotion, one word—no matter how softly spoken—could catch my ear like a gunshot. A girl sitting near the tip jar said, "Danny."

I heard her say it to her friends. Vera heard it, too. I could tell by the way she missed a step in her flight from the Rolling Rocks to the PBR and by the way she didn't make eye contact with me.

"Another round?" Vera asked the girl and her friends, even though they still had half-full bottles. She did that twice more so I wouldn't have to serve them and so that maybe they would leave sooner, before Danny showed up. After a while, they were gone.

Later, after we closed and I was restocking the coolers and Pancho was sitting in the corner shuffling the cards for rummy, Vera looked up from where she was filling out the deposit slip for the bank bag and said to me, "It's a common-enough name."

"I don't know what you're talking about," I said. But I thought to myself that Vera was right.

There are many skills involved in being a good bartender, and Vera had them all. She had a way of making me feel safe just by being near her. It seemed like nothing bad could happen while she was there, watching over us all with eyes that had seen everything already. My worries were held at bay by Vera's calmness. Even the menace of Stinky faded into the background when I was working with her. I hadn't seen Stinky since Jake ran him off, and his absence seemed sinister, like he might be lying in wait somewhere just out of sight.

But Vera, solid and comforting, made me feel braver.

"Stinky sure hasn't been around lately," I said to her later.

"And he won't be," she said. "I've permanently banned him."

"How come?" I asked, wondering if Jake had said anything.

"He told me he decided he was going to tip only every other round," Vera said. "And I told him I had decided that he could go to hell."

The Trojan War raged for nine years, and the stories of it are drenched in death. In *The Illiad*, Homer tells us that the earth streamed with blood and the funeral pyres for the fallen warriors burned continuously.

Our war was nothing like that war. Our war seemed to happen mostly inside the TV and mostly at night.

We watched the reporter on our screen, dashing in a snappy, many-pocketed vest as lights like fireworks rose in the night sky behind him. These were the Scud missiles being launched. We never saw them land—just flashes of light in the featureless dark. We never saw anyone dead. The war we saw inside our televisions every night was clean and rather quiet. It stayed inside that box.

In January, Tom got inside the box on account of an anti-war city ordinance that he was promoting to make the town a safe haven for military deserters. We watched Tom being interviewed on the ten o'clock news, talking about opposing the war. It was clear from the beginning that the television interviewer thought Tom was nuts, a traitor, a fool.

"We have no right to kill people just because they have oil and we want it," Tom said.

"What about the argument that we're bringing civilization to a barbarous people?" the TV interviewer asked. "The argument that we're bringing them peace?"

"In the nose cone of a missile?"

"Many in the United States government assure us that this will bring lasting peace to the Middle East," the interviewer said. "This will be the war to end all wars there."

"What Middle Eastern war has ever done that?" Tom asked. "The one in 1919? The one in 1920? In 1953? In 1963? The Crusades?"

The interviewer remained impassive. "Perhaps it isn't particularly useful to dwell on the past," he said. "Nineteen sixty-three is awfully ancient history. The president assures us that this war will usher in a new age of peace and prosperity for the region."

"We will bomb the world into peace?" Tom asked.

"Can you explain for our viewers why you are opposed to liberation and democracy in the Middle East?" the interviewer asked.

Over the next few days, the local newspaper featured a series of letters to the editor that fairly frothed in vitriolic indignation at Tom's remarks. Most of them suggested he be imprisoned for treason or shipped back to Russia where he came from, which made Tom laugh because he was, in fact, from Kansas.

One Friday, there was a protest outside his store—a dozen or so people holding signs and American flags and singing "Onward, Christian Soldiers" in the cold sunshine. It was organized by one of the local churches. My ex-neighbor Orla was in the little crowd of protestors, holding one end of a banner that said, "Psalm 109: 9–13." Her husband, Lem, was one of three people kneeling on the sidewalk, eyes closed and hands clasped in fervent prayer. They had planted themselves directly in front of the Che poster—"Better to die standing than to live on your knees." We watched them out the front windows of Tia's.

"What's Tom doing?" Charlie Blue asked, coming out of the kitchen and wiping his hands on a dishtowel.

"He brought them coffee awhile ago," Jake said, "but they wouldn't even talk to him. Then he had to leave to take Rosalita to a checkup. I'm watching the store for him."

We all looked at him.

"What?" Jake said. "I can see the store from here. Nobody's going in there now anyway."

"What does 'Psalm 109: 9–13' mean?" Rafi asked.

Pancho closed his eyes and in a deep, solemn voice recited, "Let his children be fatherless, and his wife a widow. Let his children be continually vagabonds, and beg; let them seek their bread also out of their desolate places. Let the extortioner catch all that he hath; and let the strangers spoil his labor. Let there be none to extend mercy unto him, neither let there be any to favor his fatherless children. Let his posterity be cut off; and in the generation following let their name be blotted out."

"Jesus!" Rafi said, sounding surprised—maybe because people were actually praying for Tom's death out in front of his store or maybe because Pancho could apparently quote Bible verses extensively, a talent formerly kept hidden.

"I looked it up earlier," Pancho said.

"Jesus," Rafi said again.

We watched them until dinnertime, when they packed up and went away.

♥♥♥

The war started to come home to me now in a way that it hadn't back when Hank had taken to wearing his army jacket in the summer heat. Now the low-scudding clouds of winter seemed ominous, and the feeble, winter-gray daylight had a waiting quality to it, like it was just barely holding at bay the flocks of Stymphalian birds that would be let loose on us as soon as the sun set. I thought I could feel them waiting for us behind the sky. I thought of Pancho lying on the dock staring up at the sky.

Sometimes it was frightening to be in the bookstore. Tom had become a lightning rod. Every day, irate people drove by and yelled things out of their car windows or came into the store itself, angry or sullen or righteous. He met them with an equanimity that often just enraged them more. He said he relished the opportunity for conversation. But at the end of the day, he sometimes came into the Cave for a beer, and his eyes looked very, very tired. Some of the professors stopped sending their students to the Hammer and Sickle for their textbooks. Tom spent so much money that month repairing broken windows in the store that he had to have a special meeting with his loan officer at the bank to get the money to pay the glass company. I began to think he was awfully brave.

Stinky drove by and shouted just about every day, but as far as I know he never had the nerve to go in and speak to Tom face to face. He must have done his drinking at one of his other regular bars because he never tried to come back into the Cave. Hank never mentioned Stinky's name and was always carefully quiet if anyone else did. He knew that Vera was keeping a suspicious eye on him, and he made sure to tip well and to keep his mouth shut.

Socrates says that the entrance to the cave is a long way up from the place where the prisoners are kept. The tunnel is dark and gets darker and colder the farther the freed prisoner travels from the fire. For a long time, he only gropes his way through. The freed prisoner keeps going forward, though, feeling his way in the darkness. Socrates doesn't tell us why. It must be a lonely time and a frightening one for the prisoner. But perhaps he understands that there is no other way out.

I started to feel it was part of my job to protect Tom, although I wasn't sure how to go about doing that, other than sitting around on the couch in the bookstore and waiting for something to happen. I wasn't the only one, it seemed, who felt this way, and one or two of us were almost always hanging around the store. Although we didn't come right out and say it to each other, our paranoia was getting to us, and conversations that seemed casual weren't casual at all.

"I thought I'd just go over to Tom's for a while," Charlie Blue would say during the lull between lunch and happy hour. And we would watch out the plate-glass window of Tia's until he came back. And then, not too much later, Jake would get up and stretch and not say anything to anybody but would amble across the street and disappear inside the bookstore door. Or just about at Tom's regular closing time, Rafi and Vera would exchange a look and Rafi would head out the back door and reappear awhile later.

"Everything okay?" Vera would nonchalantly ask, and Rafi would nod and she would try to look like she hadn't been worried.

I was sitting on the front steps of the bookstore one morning at opening time when Tom drove up in his beat-up old car. He smiled with his kind, tired eyes when he saw me.

"It's sweet," he said, "and I appreciate it." His voice was soft, and he reached out a hand to help me up. "But you-all don't have to watch over me, you know."

"I know," I said. But I went into the bookstore after him anyway and stayed there all morning.

To cheer us all up, Rafi started making a special after-work drink at the Cave that involved running a pint of rum through the coffee maker to heat it up and then mixing in sugar and a squirt of lemon juice from a lemon-shaped plastic bottle he kept in a corner of the cooler. The warm steam from the rum would hit all the soft tissues in your mouth and nose and make them tingle before you even took a drink, and the lemon juice cut the coffee-maker grease almost completely. After we locked the doors at night, we would whip up a batch and sit together at the corner table and close our eyes and sip slowly and sigh.

I sat next to Danny, leaning into him, not even playing cards but just watching the game and shooting the breeze. We talked about various things: the worst beer we ever drank and the best place to drink it, the time Pancho accidentally peed on an electric fence, possible names for Tom's baby, Greek mythology, what we would like to eat right now if only someone would bring it to us.

"If one of y'all would go get it for me, I wouldn't mind a nice dish of Blossom's homemade peach ice cream right now," Vera said.

"Brr, too cold for that," Danny said. "I want something warm—a nice big plate of barbecue."

"No barbecue places are open at this time of night," Pancho said. "Only Clyde's."

"Charlie Blue might still be over at Tia's, and we could ask him to bring us some burritos," I said.

"No, he left early," Rafi said. "He went to our house to practice some with Billy Joe."

"Only Clyde's," Pancho said again.

"I have nothing against chicken and biscuits," I said. "That just might hit the spot."

"It'll do," Danny said, "as long as I'm not the one who has to go out into the cold to get it."

"Come on, Pancho," Rafi said. "I'll go with you to help carry it back."

Vera and Rosalita both added their orders.

"What about you, Tom?" Rafi asked. "Want anything?"

Tom was sitting next to Rosalita, one arm around her, leaning back against the wall, his eyes looking drowsy.

"Nothing for me," he said sleepily. "I've already got everything I want."

In the tunnel leading out of the cave, the freed prisoner walks for a long time in absolute darkness.

In early February, on a bitterly cold morning, our phone rang just at dawn. Danny crawled out from under the blankets and went to the kitchen to answer it. When finally he came back to the bedroom, his face was gray and his voice was shaking.

"That was Rosalita calling from the hospital," he said. "Somebody shot Tom last night. He's dead."

DISSOLUTION

THE NEXT DAYS WERE a nightmare jumble of confused newspaper reports and police statements, unanswerable questions, disbelief, sadness, and fear. They had not caught Tom's murderer, and so we didn't know why he was killed. It could have been a botched robbery—although why someone looking to steal actual money would target Tom would be beyond explanation. To be fair, it was possible that his death had nothing to do with politics or with the war or with the damning prayers of our local crusading Christians. To be fair.

On the day we buried Tom, I stood between Danny and Jake and felt the wind biting all the way through to my bones. Rosalita stood by herself at the edge of his grave and never said a word, just cried onto the raw red dirt.

Jake came back to our house with Danny and me after the funeral and sat next to Danny on our couch drinking beer, not saying anything.

"I guess y'all both knew Tom for a long time," I said tentatively.

"Years," Jake said.

Danny stared into the empty fireplace.

"What do you suppose will happen to the bookstore now?" I asked.

There was a pause. Jake glanced over at Danny and then said, "Dunno," and lapsed back into silence. Danny just kept staring straight ahead.

"Rosalita . . . ," I started, but stopped when Danny stood up suddenly.

"If you don't mind," he said in a voice a little louder than usual, "I think I want to spend some time alone now."

He didn't look at me, just took the keys and shut the door behind him. When I heard the car start outside, I looked over at Jake, who was still sitting on the couch holding his beer but not drinking it.

"Don't worry," he said. "He just needs a little space for a while. He knew Tom for a long, long time."

"Where do you think he's going?"

"He'll be back when he's ready."

But Danny didn't come back at all that evening. Jake stayed, sitting on the couch watching TV and drinking beer. Eventually I went to bed, and when I woke up the next day, Jake was gone and Danny was asleep face down on the couch with all his clothes on. I didn't ever ask Danny where he had been. It could have been anywhere.

Two days later, the president of the United States declared that the war was over and that the United States had won and that there had been almost no casualties, not counting the people who didn't, after all, really count. All across the country, there were celebrations of victory.

Down in the Cave, we watched the presidential announcement on the cable news channel. Then Rafi turned off the TV, and no one said anything.

The next day when I went to open the Cave in the middle of the afternoon, I found Pancho (who of course knew where the key was hidden) already inside. The television was on with the sound off, and by the flickering light from the screen, Pancho was playing the piano—music that sounded like lonely souls lost in the wilderness.

"Whatcha doing?" I asked him.

"Shh," he said, pressing the keys with his eyes closed. "I'm trying to touch the spirit world."

He played for a long time while I swept the floors and washed the ashtrays and opened up the pool tables. By the time I came in from the back room with the quarters from the pool tables all put neatly into their paper rolls, he was sitting at the bar drying the ashtrays for me.

"Any luck?" I asked.

"Not yet," he said, looking downcast. Then he smiled a little at me in an encouraging way. "I'll keep trying, though."

"Thank you, Pancho," I said. I figured it couldn't hurt. Maybe Tom's soul was out there somewhere, and maybe he would be happy to be in touch and to have us say hello.

How strange it must be for the other prisoners when one among their number vanishes, is taken from them. It must be terrifying at first to have their gods appear among them and lay hands on their comrade. Direct contact with the gods is a dangerous proposition in many philosophies.

And afterward, when it slowly becomes clear that he is not coming back—that he is never coming back—what do they begin to think of him? Perhaps they search their memories of him to dredge up possible sins, something that would justify and give meaning to his abduction. Or perhaps they begin to develop myths of him and to weave them into their theology, transfiguring him into one among the gods who have, at long last, come for him, their brother. Are any of them resentful—angry at being left behind? Do they begin then to plot their own escape? Plato does not tell us.

All we are told is that they stay there, shackled at the bottom of the cave. They are there waiting—endlessly, faithfully waiting—for the freed one to return.

I don't know who decided it or how it was decided that the bookstore would reopen. Vera and Blossom went in together one afternoon and cleaned up Tom's blood—and came out looking older than they did when they went in. And then we reopened the store, taking shifts in pairs because it was too hard still to be in there all alone. During those days, none of us talked much, but hardly anyone ever went home alone at night.

I stopped tending bar at the Cave then so I could work the morning shifts at the bookstore, unpacking boxes of books that Tom had ordered only days ago and sitting sadly on the couch next to Jake or Danny. Tom was everywhere in the store, his coat still hanging on the back of a door, his coffee cup, a coverless copy of *Mythology* with a bookmark at the beginning of the chapter about the Trojan War sitting on the arm of the broken-down couch on the porch. Sometimes people who didn't know he had died called and asked to speak to him.

"I'm glad," Vera said when I told her I was quitting. "Somebody should be there to make sure it stays open—somebody who knew him."

The professors who had stopped sending students in for books placed orders again now. Even some who had never known Tom or been in the store called up with orders, and their students dutifully came by, holding copies of the syllabus and looking anxious for being in a place where a murder had happened. It wasn't much, but it was enough to tide us over for the time being.

Tom's daughter was born. Rosalita named her Rigoberta, and she was called Bertie by everyone. Winter rolled into spring again, but there was no Bartenders' Ball that year. The cat Emma Goldman padded softly around, looking for something she couldn't find. I kept hearing Tom's voice—I could hear him laughing in delight. But no one played the whirling dervish music anymore, and Emma Goldman didn't dance.

The Greek underworld had a distinct geography. There were specific rivers to cross—Acheron, the river of Woe; Cocytus, the river of Lamentation; Phlegethon; Styx; and Lethe, the river of Forgetfulness. And there were different areas within the underworld where dead souls were sent—Erebus; Tartarus, where the wicked would meet their everlasting torment; and the Elysian Fields, where the good would live in eternal bliss.

Hades reigned in the underworld with Persephone (when

she was not on her summer vacation), but he did not judge the souls when they arrived. That was done by a trio of judges—Rhadamanthus, Minos, and Aeacus. After the judgment was complete, punishment was left in the hands of the Furies, who were feared because they were so just.

Tom was presumably sent straight to the Elysian Fields. He had been a generous and kindly man, so it would only be just. There was no doubt he deserved a blissful eternity.

But I worried. According to Virgil, the boatman Charon had to ferry dead souls across the river of Lamentation to arrive at the entrance to the underworld. He would consent to take only those souls who had passage money with them between their lips. I worried that this might be a problem for Tom, who had been so short of cash lately because of all the repairs to the bookstore. Without the proper fee, Charon left poor souls in a shadowy limbo outside the gates of the underworld, stranded on the far shore of Lamentation.

It seems wrong that the dead would have to pay money to get into heaven—or even to get into hell. More to the point, it seems unjust.

But perhaps on the banks of Lamentation, when the time comes, we will find all of our friends, all of us who are chronically short of cash. It would be a good place to hold the next Bartenders' Ball. Tom would be there to welcome us all with joy.

Vera never spoke about her first husband. It was known, though, that he had caused her trouble and left some deep emotional scars as souvenirs. She had not intended to ever get married again. Or even fall in love again—because it's the love that really traps you, that keeps you sticking with someone you would be better off without. Vera never meant to lose herself like that again.

But Pete—Pete had scars, too. So much so that he had given up wanting anything from the world anymore, except maybe to sit quietly at the bar and drink a beer and listen to Billy Joe play the blues. He and Vera just began talking one night. That's how it started.

After the long cold winter when Tom died, Vera and Pete decided to get married. It seemed the only thing to do—to hold on tight to each other and to promise forever.

The wedding was held at Vera's house out in the pine woods south of town. The woods themselves were still black and dreary, but inside the house it was warm from the fire in the fireplace and from all of Vera and Pete's friends standing together talking and smiling and drinking wine. Pete didn't look quite like himself, dressed up in his good suit and his tie with his hair carefully combed, but Vera looked pretty in her blue silk dress and seemed happy while she promised to love him and honor him and cherish him. Blossom openly wiped away tears; Rafi did it more furtively.

The party afterward lasted all night. People danced and Billy Joe played with Charlie Blue bashfully backing him up. Endless food kept appearing from the kitchen. It felt good to laugh together in the warm little house, but all night long I couldn't forget the dark, cold woods around us.

It was Jake who finally closed the book that Tom had been reading and put it away—not on the shelves to be sold, though, but tucked under the counter.

"Who do you think did it?" I asked him—the question we

had all been asking each other over and over for months.

"Could have been anyone," he said. "Just some loser."

"Do you think it was a botched robbery, like the police say?"

"Could have been. This place is empty enough of customers a lot of the time."

"But Tom would have just given the money to someone who needed it. Why would they shoot him?"

"Maybe they just fucked up," Jake said.

"There wouldn't have been enough money here to make it worth it. Everybody knows that."

"I guess not everybody."

"Do you think it was someone else? Something else? Something political? People were awfully bent out of shape about this war. Awfully gung-ho."

"Not enough to put their own rosy asses on the line, I notice," Jake said.

"There's a difference, though, between putting yourself at risk and gunning down an unarmed man. Plenty of fanatics would be willing to do that."

Jake considered this for a minute and then lit another cigarette.

"Do you have a theory?" he asked.

"No," I said. "Or maybe yes—too many theories. Like I can't help but think that someone like Stinky, say . . . someone who had something to prove . . . "

"I doubt that little pissant would have the guts to pull the trigger. He's never been anything other than talk."

I remembered Stinky's fingernails digging into my skin, the stench of his breath in my face, how he had started to push me down on my knees.

"See, that's the thing," I said. "It's the pissants who do it. It's the pissants who get in over their heads trying to prove something. And then things get out of hand."

"Maybe," Jake conceded. "But whoever it was, it was just some loser who fucked up."

At first, no one was ever alone in the bookstore. There was, after all, a murderer on the loose, and if you let yourself think too clearly about that, a wave of fear rolled up and the silence took on a frightening, suffocating quality of real terror. But human beings are resilient. By the time the spring sun was hot enough to open the dogwood blossoms, I was opening the store by myself in the morning quiet.

I don't know of a town in the whole South where there is an especially high demand for communist books, and after the first few weeks of mourning drew us all together there, it became clear to me that it had been Tom whom people had come to see, Tom himself who had brought people to the store, and without him, I had a lot of empty time on my hands.

The bookstore was converted from an old house. No matter how often I swept the floorboards, they always felt dusty to my bare feet. The windowpanes rippled gently and made the outside seem dreamy and unreal. The books looked permanently settled into their shelves, even where they were all jumbled together. The rooms smelled of sawdust, of old paint and paper, and—very faintly—of Tom. But that may have just been my memory fooling me.

After Bertie was born, Rosalita, who might otherwise have felt only blissful joy, felt instead despair. She pondered the Fates that could have made life otherwise, but had chosen to make it unbearably hard. She felt walls all around her, and it seemed incomprehensible to her that she had once been filled with hope and expectation. It seemed incomprehensible that she would ever feel those feelings again. She and Bertie lived in Tom's house, surrounded by all she had left of him.

It became hard for Rosalita to stay awake. She became listless and forlorn, and although the sound of the baby's crying could drag her to the side of the cradle that Billy Joe had made for her, it hurt her to look at her baby's eyes and see the ghost of Tom looking back at her from so far away. The space between the living and the dead is not a long distance, but once someone crosses it, they can never cross back.

"I'm worried about Rosalita," Blossom said to me, standing next to my table and holding the coffeepot in her hand while I ate breakfast. "That child is looking too thin for someone who has a new baby. I can tell she's not eating. Does she come into the bookstore any?"

"Not so far," I said. "Vera went by to see her yesterday, see if she needed anything, but she was asleep."

"Where are her folks?"

"I'm not sure—I think her mother is in Guatemala. And I think I heard that her daddy was disappeared. Tom was pretty much the only family she had. Other than the baby."

"A baby is one kind of family," Blossom said. "A mama is another."

She looked thoughtful, and then she shook herself. "Are you done eating those biscuits?" she asked me. "Then come with me and help me carry some things."

We went to see Rosalita with two pies, a plate of hot biscuits, and four pints of green tomato pickles. Rosalita ate a piece of pie just to humor Blossom and then felt better for it. She felt so much better, in fact, that she crawled into Blossom's arms and buried her face in the warm, vanilla-scented softness of Blossom's neck and sobbed and sobbed and sobbed. Blossom rocked her gently and let her cry.

"Oh, my baby," Blossom crooned into Rosalita's hair. "Oh, my poor, poor baby."

I heard Bertie whimpering from her cradle and went to get her and hold her in my arms. She was a serious baby with quizzical eyes. "It's going to be okay," I whispered to her, but she just looked silently back at me. I walked with her back and forth across the room, slowly swaying from side to side. "Hush, little baby, don't say a word," I sang to her. "Josie's gonna buy you a mockingbird . . . ."

We stayed a long time and left them asleep next to each other in Tom's old iron bed.

For a while after that, Blossom and I went by the house almost every evening after dinner. Blossom would sit at the kitchen table with Rosalita and drink cups of coffee and talk. I walked back and forth, back and forth across the living-room floor holding Bertie in my arms and singing every old lullaby I could think of. At first, I could remember only two or three, and I would have to sing the same ones over and over again, but eventually others started to come back to me, and I could go on and on for quite a while before I had to repeat myself. It was strange to think that my mother must have once sung these songs to me, held me in her arms like I held Bertie. I couldn't remember it, but the songs were all there, slowly making their way up out of my memory, so it must have been true.

Sometimes Bertie was wide awake and would watch my eyes intently, looking serious, like someone trying to understand Greek when they spoke only French. Other times, she would fall asleep right away, and the tender, translucent lids would cover her eyes and her long golden eyelashes would lie on her cheeks like butterfly wings, and I would keep walking back and forth so as not to wake her.

∎∎∎

I came home to find Danny sitting on the couch, watching TV and drinking beer.

"You've been gone a long time," he said. "A suspicious man would be suspicious."

"I've been with Rosalita and the baby. You know you don't need to be suspicious."

He sighed. "I know it," he said, his eyes on the TV.

"The baby is sweet," I said. And then when he didn't answer, "Don't you like babies?"

"I like babies fine—as long as they belong to someone else."

"They smell so sweet."

"Their diapers don't."

"And Bertie has the sweetest little baby fingers and little baby toes and little baby mouth."

"The better to scream the house down with, Red Riding Hood."

"You sure are grumpy tonight."

"I'm not grumpy. I'm just bored. I've been waiting here for you. Let's go out and have some fun. Let's find some people and stay up all night together and have a good time."

"Oh, honey, I'm beat and I've got to get up early tomorrow to open the store."

He didn't say anything for a minute.

"Suit yourself," he finally said. "I'll be back when I'm back."

After he left, the house was too quiet, and even though I went right to bed, I didn't fall asleep for the longest time.

The shot glasses at Tia's had white lines going all the way around them about half an inch down from the rim. When the bartenders poured shots of tequila for ordinary customers, they filled the glasses to the white line. When they poured shots for us, they filled the glasses to the brim. Some of us drank tequila with lime and salt that we licked off the curve between the thumb and forefinger. But most of us didn't bother with that. We just knocked the shots back in one gulp, without ceremony. People settling in for the evening would slow themselves down by drinking a beer between shots of tequila. It was possible to build up an amazing tolerance, but you had to work at it steadily.

But people who wanted to reach oblivion more quickly could sit at the bar at Tia's and drink tequila so fast that by the time they started to feel it, they had already had enough to knock them out. Unconsciousness could be a relief sometimes. And there was always someone around who would take you home and sling you into your bed—or near enough to it.

Danny and I started to argue more and more that spring. The more we argued, the more tequila seemed to me to be a good escape.

"Ease up, sugar," Danny said to me. "You're drinking like your own ghost is chasing you."

"I want to go fast," I said. "I want to be there already now."

"You need to slow down some—just take it easy and make it last. Let's just enjoy the evening."

"Why? Why do I have to slow down? Why don't you speed up instead?"

"Life doesn't have to be as hard as you make it, Josie. You'd be happier if you would just take it as it comes. You would be happier if you would just relax."

"I think *you* would be the one who would be happier if I would just relax."

He laughed. "You say it like it's a bad thing. Don't you want me to be happy?"

"All I want right now is not to have to think about anything anymore or feel anything anymore or want anything anymore."

"Oh, sugar, be very, very careful what you wish for."

"I'm not too interested, as a rule, in being careful. You should know that by now. I'm the same person I've always been."

"Are you?" he said, grabbing my hand.

"Oh, Lord," I said. "Don't start. This conversation is starting to bore the crap out of me."

"You and me both," he sighed. "I'm worn out and I guess I'm just going home. Do you want to come?"

I went home with him, but I fell asleep before he came to bed, and when I woke up in the morning, he was already gone.

"You're gone an awful lot," I said to Danny, "and you're not always at work. Who are you spending all this time with? Is there someone else?"

"God, I hate suspicious women! Of course, there's not someone else."

There was someone else. Her name was Tawni, and she was pretty in the same way my cousin Belle was. It wasn't that Danny flirted with her at the bar at the café—it was that he so pointedly didn't. And that she was always there these days. And that she seemed so obviously conscious of me whenever I was around.

And that I got the feeling I was interrupting something.

The most fun part of figuring out that the relationship you had managed to fool yourself into thinking might, against all odds, last forever, but was now over, was getting to choose between being a harpy and being a doormat. I myself alternated between the two, to stunningly schizophrenic effect. Danny took to staying out late—even by his standards—which meant that I didn't see him at all most nights. I would sometimes find him asleep in bed when I came home from the bookstore in the late afternoons and would sometimes *not* find him, but would go and feel his toothbrush in the bathroom to see if it was damp, if maybe he had been home and gone.

When he was home, we circled around the same argument.

"I never lied to you," Danny said. "I never made promises."

"You did!" I screamed. "You made me believe things that weren't true!"

"I never said them!"

"You can say things without using words!"

"I'm not going to have this conversation with you!" he shouted, and then slammed the door and was gone.

The house in the woods was cold and lonesome without him, and I went back to spending my evenings keeping Rafi company down in the Cave. Pancho sat next to me from time to time and just shook his head sorrowfully.

"It'll pass, honey," Rafi would say, pushing another free beer my way. He was trying his best to keep me continuously drunk. For medicinal reasons.

"Oh, Rafi," I would say. "The weeks go on and on."

I wanted it to be done. I knew the end of me and Danny was inevitable. But the truth, of course, is that just because some new girl comes along, it doesn't mean that you stop loving the girl you live with, that you stop sleeping next to her (sometimes) or passing her in the kitchen in the late-afternoon light, seeing all the little pieces of her you fell in love with in the first place. You can still be tender to her and share secrets with her and love her, the whole time you're betraying her. The problem isn't that now there's a new girl—the problem is that now there are *two* girls, and the one you love the most is the one you're going to hurt. The new girl, well, she's *new.* And the old girl, the one whose secrets you already know so well, the one you've loved a long time now, she doesn't stand a chance. ("Lay your sleeping head, my love, Human on my faithless arms.")

I knew all that. Knowledge, however, did not make me any more reconciled to the facts. Knowledge did not make me reasonable or serene.

Danny and I didn't even fight anymore at the end. "We've already had every fight there is to be had," Danny said.

On the day I moved out of our little house in the woods, I went down to the Cave and sat at the bar, not even drinking the beer Rafi put down in front of me.

"You probably don't want to hear a speech about how it is better to have loved and lost, I'm guessing," Rafi said.

"Not really."

He was quiet for a while, letting me brood.

"It can be nice to be alone," he said.

"But only if you choose it—not if you don't have a choice."

"You always have a choice," he said, not looking at me. "You do."

So I stayed there, sitting at the far end of the bar all evening while he worked. There was no band that night, but it was busy anyway, and Rafi and I didn't talk. We didn't talk after last call or while he restocked the coolers and I covered up the pool tables. Vera and Pete stopped by to get the bank bag, but they didn't stay, and there was no one else around. Rafi turned off the lights, and it was so quiet I could hear my own heartbeat.

The windows at Tia's were mostly dark when we walked together out to my car, but we could tell by the faint glow coming from the back that the dishwashers weren't quite done yet. It was still early by bar time—not even 3 A.M. I unlocked the passenger-side door of my car for Rafi, but it was too dark to see him lean over to unlock my door from the inside. I heard the click when he did.

We still didn't talk while we drove to his house. Sometimes it is impossible to say things. When we were standing together under the trees in his driveway, he took my hand and led me silently into the house, through the dark kitchen and the hallway into his bedroom. I pushed the door shut behind us.

Then I kissed Rafi. He backed me against the closed bedroom door and put his arms around me. His lips were warm. We kissed again. In the moonlight from the open window, I could see his bed, rumpled sheets, a pillow on the floor.

"This is a mistake," he whispered into my ear. "You'll end up breaking my heart."

"Let's not think about anything right now," I said. "Let's just go to bed, and we can think about things in the morning."

We sat on his bed, kissing. I touched his face with the tips of my fingers.

"So I'm your rebound," he said.

"Maybe. Does it really matter so much?"

I lay down on the sheets, and he lay down next to me.

"Did you really love Danny?" he asked.

"Danny . . . ," I started to say, but then I couldn't go on because I realized I was sobbing.

Rafi pulled me close in his arms, and I pressed my face against his neck. I didn't want to cry, but I couldn't stop. Rafi held me for a long time.

My head was still on his chest when I woke up in the morning. He was awake, looking tired in the blue morning light.

"Are we still friends?" I asked.

"Always."

I dropped him at Blossom's, but didn't feel like eating anything, so I went on to the bookstore to open up.

That afternoon, I moved into Pete's three-room shotgun house down by the river, empty since he married Vera and moved all his stuff to her place. It was called a "shotgun" because the rooms and doors were all lined up so that if you shot a gun in the front door, the bullet would go straight through the house to the back door without (theoretically) hitting anything on the way. Fortunately no one ever tried it.

It's important to have friends when you are miserable, and you should count yourself especially lucky if you are fortunate enough to have generous friends with access to a bottomless supply of free alcohol. At times like this, a sufficient amount of tequila, for example, can lead you to a philosophical state of mind where the renunciation of your former one true love seems not only possible but even morally pure and elevated, and you forget that you can't really renounce someone who has already dumped you—or at least not with much actual effect on him. And if this superior mental state of dignified refusal is expressed mostly by slurring "Fuck him—fuck the fucker" repeatedly to anyone who will listen and then throwing up wretchedly onto your own shoes, that does not negate the overall effect, which is to make you feel so *physically* bad in the morning that you don't have enough energy or brain cells left to spend on contemplating how *emotionally* bad you feel, since you have to spend all your effort on trying not to move or to smell anything. Surprisingly soon, however, you will want a cigarette, and having smoked all of yours in the orgy of sodden desolation the night before, you will have to bum one from your friends. They will give you cigarettes out of their packs, even if they have only two left. This generosity will remind you of what great friends you have, and—especially if you are medicating your tequila hangover with Bloody Marys—this will make you cry.

It's probably best just to get it all out of your system at once.

This was not my best period. The specter of Danny's previous girlfriend Candy returned sometimes to whisper late-night suggestions of spurned-lover craziness and mayhem. I felt now that perhaps I had judged Candy too harshly, back in the days when I was innocently shocked and amazed that anyone would think that making such an ugly spectacle of herself would serve any positive purpose. Now, making an ugly spectacle of myself, to my more experienced and worldly eye, seemed to be a perfectly reasonable plan of action. If I couldn't have Danny back, at least I could irritate the crap out of him. It was better than nothing.

Rafi counseled against this plan. His line of argument, renewed every day across the bar at the Cave, had two themes. The first was that Danny wasn't worth it, and—when that failed under the unassailable counterargument of "But I loooove him"—the second was that I should have another beer first. This second argument was usually successful, although often rather messy, and Vera and Rafi and Pancho had to take turns getting me home and into bed. There is enormous comfort to be had in friends who see the worst of you and do not turn away. "We've all been there," Rafi would shrug nonchalantly when I turned up looking woeful and contrite every afternoon. He and I did not kiss again, but I thought about him sometimes, thought about the rumpled sheets on his bed and how warm his lips were against mine.

My friends did other things in their own ways to make me feel better. Vera scolded me—in the best imitation of a mother she could manage—to "toughen up, buttercup." It wasn't, truth be told, such a bad approximation of a mother, if your mother happened to, say, work in a lumber camp. Or as a stevedore. Anyway it was more helpful than any advice my actual mother had ever bothered to give me. Billy Joe sat next to me at the bar and made drily disparaging comments about Tawni. Charlie Blue made a point of telling me every stupid joke he heard in the kitchen at Tia's or could remember from elementary school. This gave me some comfort.

JAKE

JAKE WAS SITTING ON THE COUCH in the bookstore, reading Walt Whitman. It was late morning, already a scorcher. No one else was around.

"Jake," I said. He looked up. "Did you ever have a broken heart?"

"Hasn't everyone?"

"Have they? How do they recover? How does anyone ever get over it?"

He thought about it for a minute.

"Well, you just do, don't you? You just keep going on day after day, and eventually you find out you're over it."

"But suppose you don't? Suppose you never do? Suppose you don't even want to?"

"I'm not sure you have a choice in the matter. You might think you can decide how you will feel about someone or how long you will remember them. But in the end, it's just a matter of fate what stays with you and what goes."

"What stayed with you?"

"When?"

"When you had a broken heart."

"What makes you think I've had only one?"

"How many, then? How many women have managed to break your heart?"

"My fair share," he said, turning back to his book.

"Enough that you've developed a remedy?" I persisted.

"You should know as well as I do that the only remedy for a broken heart is another broken heart," he said. "All the poets in the world swear by it as a sure-fire cure. Poets must know. Now let me read—somebody may come in and want to buy this book someday."

"Doubtful," I said. "Customers are not exactly breaking down the doors lately. Even the textbook orders are drying up."

He didn't answer and we sat silently. He was reading and I was looking out the window. After a while, I got up and got a book of Sylvia Plath poetry off the shelves and came back to the couch. He looked up and cocked an eyebrow at me.

"Poets must know," I said.

"Well," he said, "maybe not that one."

I laughed.

Jake stayed at the store all day and was still there when I locked up at dinnertime.

"Are you going home?" he asked me.

"I guess," I sighed. "Might as well—I can't think of anywhere else I ought to go."

"Come with me. Let's go for a drive."

"Where to?"

"Nowhere. Nowhere in particular."

I considered it. "Nowhere sounds like the perfect place," I said.

We drove out on the highway heading south. We drove until we hit the state line and only then turned around to come back. By the time he dropped me off at home, I was tired and finally able to go to sleep.

Jake and I took to going out for drives in the countryside, speeding down deserted stretches of lonely back roads, going nowhere as fast as we could, Jake driving with a beer in one hand and me leaning back in the passenger seat with my feet up on the dashboard. At dusk, with a storm coming in from the east, our headlights hit the speed-limit signs out on the old highway, making them glow silver against the luminous gray sky. The signs were beautiful, like strange pearls, as we blew past them going ninety miles an hour.

The best thing about Jake was that he was sad when I was sad. Of course, Jake was always kind of sad. One of his endearing qualities, in fact, was that he had absolutely no charm. Given my recent experience with a charming man, this was awfully appealing to me just then.

"Whatever happened to that old church lady you used to live next to?" Rafi asked me one afternoon while we were sitting together whiling away the hours.

"I don't have any idea," I said. "I never see her anymore."

But speak of the devil, they say, and the devil appears. I don't know how Orla got my new address and found me at my little shotgun haven down by the river. And I certainly don't know why she felt she should come visit me, but it wasn't too long after I moved in than there was a knock on the door, and there stood Orla on my tiny front porch, wearing a rigid smile on her snapping-turtle face and carrying a bag of canned goods.

"Hello!" she called out, coming straight in the door when I opened it. "I was cleaning out my cupboards and found these— you might want to be careful of the ones that are a little swollen. Anyway I was sure you would need some things." She glanced around my tiny living room with a beady, critical eye. "Now that you're alone again," she said cheerily.

She handed me the bag with the air of a strict nursery governess who knew what was best for me but was cagey enough not to say it to my face. She would get her way in the end, she was certain.

Orla looked around the room for somewhere to sit and finally chose the very front edge of a straight-backed wooden chair.

"Have a seat," I said.

"So I see you never got married," she said.

"No," I said, blushing. "No."

"Well, I guess that's not surprising," she said. "You know what they say about getting the milk for free!"

"Would you like some tea?" I said, desperate to get out of the room.

"Oh, no," she said. "Just a Coke."

"I'll see if I have any," I said, and went into the kitchen.

Orla, however, followed me, taking in the disheveled state in one comprehensive survey. "Hmm," she said, pursing her lips.

I scrabbled around in the refrigerator, hoping that a Coke might possibly appear but knowing it wouldn't. "I don't have any Cokes," I said, somehow shamefaced. "I have orange juice?"

"Oh, no," she said. "I don't want that!"

She looked expectantly at me, and I dove back into the refrigerator as if I could somehow conjure up an acceptable beverage out of the jars of canned tomatoes and cold Clyde's Chicken languishing there. No luck.

"A glass of water?" I asked.

"No," Orla said with an air of resignation but no surprise. "I'll just have to do without."

She headed back into the living room and sat on the edge of a different chair, dusting it off a little with her hand first. She stared at me for a few minutes, as if expecting me to tell her why I had called her there.

"Well, I have lots of news," she said, and launched into a long tale of Lem's annual colonoscopy.

I gasped in faux sympathy and said "How awful!" at random places in the story. This went on for quite a while. "Oh, dear," I said, shaking my head and wishing I was having a conversation I cared about.

"Well, I've got to go," Orla finally said. "I can't stay any longer—I'm so busy, you know. But I knew that I had better bring you some things you would need. Next time, I'll have to bring you some Cokes!" She laughed a dry little laugh of disparagement.

I thanked her for the canned goods until she finally seemed satisfied enough with my appreciation and headed down the front steps.

"I knew you wouldn't get married," she called out gaily across the yard, waving her hand goodbye and smiling.

Eventually the freed prisoner glimpses daylight—his first sight of the light from the sun—glimmering at the end of the tunnel. Initially it seems to be just a pinpoint of light, and he might be unsure if it is real, so faint, so far away. He might think it a star, if he had any knowledge of stars. On his lonely journey without the comrades of his former life, he has no one to help him puzzle it out, no one to help him build myths and ideologies out of this light. The freed prisoner must make sense of the world from only his own observations.

So he advances, guiding his steps by a star whose meaning he must construct on his own.

If there is a difference between the myths we believe in along with all of our comrades and the myths that are only our own, known to ourselves alone, it is that our shared myths are spoken out loud. They gather authority and solidity from the confirmation of others. They have substance—the substance of our comrades' beliefs. They are real.

We do not often speak out loud of our own private myths. They are merely daydreams. But we are still guided by their star.

***

"You're spending a lot of time with Jake lately," Vera said to me one afternoon.

"I guess so."

"I thought you didn't like him too much."

"He's okay—no big deal."

"Does Danny know?"

"Why should I care anymore about what Danny knows? He's got about all he can handle with his new girlfriend."

Vera went on, "Be that as it may, Danny and Jake have been friends for a long time."

"All Jake and I do is go for drives in the country," I said. I didn't tell her how Jake had held my hand while we picked our way gingerly through the ruined rooms of the abandoned cotton mill off the highway in Magnolia, or how we had kissed each other in the katydid-laced silence of the empty spinning room with the summer bees zooming in and out through the broken windows.

"Is it really over with you and Danny?" Vera asked.

"Apparently so."

Vera sighed. "It just seemed to me that you made a good couple," she said. "It seemed that you each gave the other one something you needed."

"Well, Danny's getting what he needs elsewhere now."

"And are you?"

"Am I what?"

"Getting what you need elsewhere now?"

"I don't need anything except another beer."

Vera pulled one up from the cooler. "If you say so," she said.

Finally one night, home after a long drive to nowhere, Jake and I found ourselves undressing one another in the dark of my bedroom.

"I thought we didn't like each other," I said, only half joking. "Why are we doing this?"

"You're doing this because you're a sucker for lost causes," Jake said. "You can't help yourself."

He pulled me close. I kissed him on the ear, then the side of the neck, then his shoulder.

"What about you?" I whispered. "Why are you doing this?"

"Because I've wanted to kiss you ever since the very first time I saw your mouth."

Billy Joe, as both a carpenter and a guitar player who played the blues late at night in dim, smoky bars, naturally had his pick of women. Once, he took the stage with a bandage wrapped around his left hand where he'd gotten himself with a nail gun earlier in the day, and a girl in the front of the audience actually fainted from lust. She said it was the heat, but we all knew what she meant. And Billy Joe was not the sort of cold-blooded person who would let a pretty girl faint from lust and not come to her aid. And also, possibly, the aid of her pretty friends as well.

But a man has plenty of time to think when he's hammering together wall braces day after day. And when that same man spends his evenings playing the blues—songs about broken hearts and broken lives and love and loneliness and longing—his thoughts naturally take a turn toward deeper questions. And despite being constantly besieged by lusting girls, Billy Joe was a thoughtful man. So when a woman came along who was different, Billy Joe fell in love with her.

We started seeing less of Billy Joe. He and Lily (that was her name) stayed at home a lot of nights, watching TV together or just hanging around talking or sitting on her porch swing together while Billy Joe picked out tunes on his guitar. When he played the Cave, girls still came around, but now he seemed not to see them. And when they obtruded themselves into his notice, a little imploring, a little frustrated, he didn't ever focus his full attention on them anymore. It was as if he were always thinking of something else. He dismissed them not like a man reluctantly renouncing his former—now, alas, forbidden—pleasures, but like a connoisseur in a crowded museum, craning his neck to see around the hordes of loudmouthed tourists so as to keep his eyes on the masterpiece.

Gradually Billy Joe stopped sleeping at the little white house with the stones in the frying pan in the kitchen that he had shared so long with Rafi. He started going straight to Lily's house after work, although at first he just kept his toothbrush there. But then his books and his clothes and then his guitars migrated over. When Rafi cooked breakfast in the early afternoon, Billy Joe wasn't there anymore to share it. Although sometimes he stopped by the Cave after closing time and gave Rafi a ride home, he only dropped Rafi off and then went on to Lily's house to sleep.

Despite this, Rafi liked Lily. We all did. She was warm and smart and had bright laughing eyes. The day after Billy Joe asked Lily to marry him, he and Rafi took the pan of river stones out into the woods behind their house. They stayed out there a long time, and Rafi told me later that they had thrown all the stones, one by one, as deep as they could into the trees.

Billy Joe and Lily found a tin-roofed house out on the old highway toward Millboro, and Rafi found a place to rent downtown.

"Are you going to be okay?" I asked Rafi.

"Sure," Rafi said. "Love is a good thing, even if it's not your own."

In *Symposium*, the companion of Socrates named Phaedrus argues that Love gives us the greatest good because he is one of the most ancient gods. Even before Gaia, the earth, existed, according to the legends there was Love. Love is so ancient that he has no father or mother, Phaedrus tells his companions, quoting the myths that are history.

But one god existed before Love—Chaos. Chaos was the first of them all, preceding everything. He is the foundation upon which we are all built. But Chaos is not the father of

Love—Love has no parents. Neither are they siblings. Perhaps they are old comrades or old rivals. Perhaps they view each other with the jaundiced eyes of ancient generals who have gone through countless campaigns together.

But no matter the ultimate power of Love, it is important to remember that Chaos was there first.

Jake was living then in a two-room house in a patch of weeds behind Blossom's restaurant. He'd moved there after Danny left to live with me. It was considered a step up from Boystown. It had once been part of the servants' quarters of the big house owned by the mill foreman. The big house had fallen down and been carted off bit by bit in the years after the mill stopped working, but Jake said his house was fortunately already too close to the ground to fall any farther down.

Jake didn't have much furniture—just a mattress on the floor with two pillows and the brown vinyl backseat of a dismantled sedan for a sofa. The walls had all been painted blue so many years ago that they were no longer just one color but ran the gamut from the color of clouds to the color of hard summer afternoon skies to the color of blue jays. There was no kitchen in the little house, although Jake had a dangerous-looking hot plate. He mostly ate at Blossom's, sitting in the back with all her children and doing dishes for a while afterward.

Because it was so conveniently located, we slept at Jake's house pretty often. He didn't have any curtains on his windows, and we could see the moon from bed.

Rosalita eventually came back to the bookstore, bringing Bertie with her, stepping gingerly in through the door. Blossom came with her.

Pancho and I were sitting on the couch when they showed up. We got up and stood in the middle of the floor, not saying anything. Rosalita stood just inside the door, looking all around.

"It seems strange to me that all of this is still here," she finally said. She walked over to the Liberation Theology section and ran her fingers gently across the spines of the books. "*Qué extraño.*" She turned and looked at us. "I thought it all would have disappeared."

Bertie gurgled happily and reached out at the shiny colors of the book jackets. "Ba!" she said, and waved her hands in the air.

"It's still here," I said.

"We're still here," Pancho said.

Rosalita turned and looked all around the store again.

"Take your time," Blossom said to her. "You don't need to decide anything right now unless you want to. When you're ready to come back, everything will be here."

"Ba! Ba! Ba!" Bertie said, laughing her bubbly baby laugh. Rosalita smiled down at her.

"*Creo que . . . ,*" Rosalita said. "I think that it is time to come back."

"We're here," Pancho said again.

Rosalita spread Bertie's baby quilt on the floor in front of the couch. Bertie sat in the middle of it.

"Ba!" she said.

"Yes," Rosalita said. "We're here."

The nicest thing about getting dumped by Danny was that I never had to see his parents again. Or any other parents, for that matter. It's safe to say that when Jake thought about home— the house where he had grown up—and about his parents and his brothers, there was no butter yellow Cadillac in his mind, no crocheted cats, no protecting eyes of Jesus. His family was from up in the hills like mine, where most people are hard up against it and where cheap alcohol is sometimes the only way to make it through, even if it's the thing that eventually drives you crazy. Jake's dad was one of the ones who had not made it through. According to the autopsy, his blood alcohol content was so high that it was amazing he had the wherewithal to even start a car, much less navigate it off the side of a mountain. But by that time, he had been gone so long from their lives that Jake said neither he nor any of his brothers even cared.

Jake didn't think it was alcohol per se that made his mother crazy. He thought it was probably more just the awful loneliness after his dad took off and left her with six boys under the age of ten. She was too worn out to find another man and too despair- ing to even want to anymore. She started talking to herself and cashing the WIC checks at the liquor store. One bright Sunday morning, she put on every single dress she had and went to church to tell them all about what Jesus had been saying to her. That afternoon, she was admitted to the state mental hospital in Delphia, and the boys were divided up among the various rela- tives in the area. Being tougher than they looked, most of them grew up to be okay.

The first Thursday of every month was visiting day, and Jake would dutifully make the drive to Delphia to visit his mother. Then he would come back and drink himself blind.

It rained a lot that summer. Some people, claiming special knowledge from Native American ancestors, blamed it on a weather cycle that naturally repeated, they said, every seven years, with an especially wet summer the seventh year of every seventh cycle, of which this apparently was one. Some people blamed it on global warming and tried to convince their friends to stop driving their cars and to walk everywhere instead. This met with minimal success, owing mostly to all the rain. A preacher at a big church in town gave a Sunday sermon saying that it was the fault of all the homosexuals, and the very next day the rain came down so hard that it opened a big sinkhole in the church's parking lot that swallowed up the preacher's new Mercedes. He went on the radio and said that such an incident just proved his point, but we didn't see how. People laughed at him so much that eventually he had to move to Oklahoma.

Water in all the creeks kept rising, and by the time the weather cleared up, I was pretty much drowning in Jake.

"Just keep kissing me until I can't think about anything else," I said to him. "I don't want to be able to think about anything except you."

"Troubled by ghosts?"

"Maybe it's the rain that brings them out."

"Maybe it's just the nature of ghosts," he said. "If they were willing to stay buried, they wouldn't be ghosts in the first place."

"Don't talk—kiss me!"

"It won't be enough."

"We can never be sure until we try."

For a long time, Jake was only my cure for a broken heart. He and I didn't expect too much from each other—it was the basis of our relationship.

Everything changed the day we killed the squirrel. We were driving on the back road by the old mill. No one ever drove on that road after the mill shut down. Everyone who had worked there had to commute thirty miles to Dunn every day to a new mill that passed all the OSHA inspections but was still a living hell. We passed only one car going the other way—it was a long white Cadillac, and we remarked on it at the time.

And then we saw the squirrel. It was in the opposite lane. It had been hit but not killed. And it was trying very hard not to die, holding its head up and dragging its broken body across the hot blacktop by its front paws. Its back paws were mangled and bloody, and we could hear through the open car windows that the squirrel was crying—a weeping, choking sound that mingled with the drone of the katydids and the *shush*ing sound of the mill river.

Jake stopped the car and we got out. The squirrel seemed not to even notice us as we got closer and closer. Its eyes were fixed straight ahead, staring at the tall grass at the edge of the road, where another squirrel, tense and watchful, stood poised, terrified of us and yet unwilling to leave his friend—wanting to flee but staying. The squirrel in the road kept crying and trying to drag himself forward, but he wasn't moving much now, and the blood from his legs was starting to bake on the hot asphalt.

Jake was different then, in that moment, than he had been before.

"You know what we have to do, don't you?" he asked me.

We got back in the car. Jake was steady behind the wheel and crushed the squirrel's head cleanly at great speed.

We stopped the car a hundred yards down the road and walked back in the sudden quiet to make sure he was dead and not suffering anymore. The other squirrel still sat by the side of the road, not tense and poised for flight anymore—just sitting, silent and resigned.

Jake held my hand, and from then on things were different between us. For one thing, we stopped looking for death on the highways, having found enough of it. And for another thing, we had a secret now that we never told anybody else. But the most important thing was that I had seen Jake's act of terrible compassion. I had seen how he hated to do it and how he made himself do it anyway, and he could never, after that, be just another boy to me.

The next day, we went back to that spot by the mill because I felt, even though it was foolish, that we should bring flowers to what was now a grave. It took us a long time to find enough wildflowers growing by the side of the road.

"There's no such thing as heaven or hell, you know," Jake said to me. "Gone is gone."

"I know," I said, but we went anyway.

The squirrel's body was stretched out on the pavement. And next to it, another squirrel lay, curled up on its side, dead. Not a mark was on its body. We covered them both with the flowers and went away.

I really hadn't paid all that much careful attention to Jake before, in the early days when he was just Danny's sidekick—always there, but still somehow apart from everyone else. But now I couldn't pay attention to anyone else. It was like all the best parts of falling in love at long last with an old friend and falling in love at first sight with a total stranger. Now Jake was mesmerizing to me. Maybe it was only the rebound from Danny. Or maybe Danny was only the prelude to Jake.

If you saw Jake around town and didn't know him, you might not think too highly of him. He washed dishes in restaurants here and there and never had much cash. He drank too much and brooded in ways that weren't pretty. He wasn't handsome in any conventional sense, and the clothes he got at the Salvation Army thrift store made him look like an accountant gone to seed. He was none too clean. Whatever romantic dreams he may once have had were long gone by then.

But if you got to know Jake, eventually he began to seem different from those first impressions. You started to see all the kindness that was in him, all the sweetness he had never lost, even with all he had been through. You could sit around in Jake's house and he didn't expect you to necessarily talk to him if you didn't feel like it. You could lie on his bed and just read a book while he sat on the couch reading, too, and if you fell asleep, when you woke up he would still be there and would smile at you when he saw that your eyes were open. On clear mornings, he would kind of stumble into the bookstore when it first opened and nobody else was around. He didn't ever say it, but he was always hoping that Rosalita would be there with Bertie. If she wasn't, he would go off for coffee at Blossom's pretty soon. But if she was, it was like someone lit a tiny candle deep inside him, and Jake would take Bertie carefully in his arms and hold her close and walk with her all around the inside of the store, talking to her about all the books and the people on the posters, and then he would walk with her all around the outside of the store, talking to her about the trees and the birds and the cars going past on Thornapple Street. Jake didn't seem quite so terribly apart then. Bertie would look at his face and babble and coo, and Jake would look back at her and answer as if she had spoken. Sometimes he told her things about Tom, stories and memories. "Now your daddy," he would always begin, "was a very good man . . . ."

There is no doubt that the men in our little world loved each other. In their world made of the bars and the clubs and Boystown and the nighttime, the friendships among the men were powerful, and such women as managed to work our way in were always a little bit on probation, tolerated but never allowed to break the bond the boys had forged long ago during nights of mythical wildness that had happened before we ever came around. The boys had driven bad cars fast across the Mojave Desert together and had fallen in love with sisters in Mexico together and had spent nights in jail together. It was the job of the girls to listen to the tales and marvel. We had not been there.

Danny and Jake were best friends and had done all these things, the two of them together. And I had lived with Danny. But now there was Jake.

It was inevitable what would happen. In the battered morning light, ragged and rough edged from too much night, Jake and I snuck in the side door of Blossom's and huddled together at the very back table, smoking the last of our cigarettes in the slowly fading dawn. Blossom herself had seen it all too often before to be surprised. She brought us coffee and understanding.

And then Danny came in.

His eyes locked not with mine but with Jake's. It was Jake, after all, who had broken the code of men and betrayed him.

That afternoon, Danny broke up with Tawni and then went and drank at Tia's until Charlie Blue had to carry him home in a heap. Like Jake had told me long ago, Danny was a romantic man.

HELL

10

HOW BRAVE THE FREED PRISONER must have been, coming to the end of the tunnel and stepping out into the sunlight so bright that it blinds him. It must have been like stepping off the edge of the world, unable to see, into an abyss. Plato tells us that after a whole life spent in the gentle glow of firelight, the glare of the sun is overwhelming, devastating to the senses. At first, the prisoner is dazzled by the brilliance of the light above and squints his eyes against it in pain and fear. Yet even in his blindness, the prisoner dares to step forward into the empty air.

He is at this moment braver than any of the philosophers who are waiting to greet him or any of the gods who engineered this game. The philosophers and gods know what awaits in the world above the cave. There is nothing uncertain there for them. They have nothing to fear. But the prisoner, sightless and alone, knows nothing. And knowing nothing of what will become of him, he nevertheless, after one final moment of hesitation, takes his hand away from the rough rock wall of the tunnel and, as his fingertips lose contact with the last reminder of his whole world, walks into the void.

Yes, how brave he must have been—how much more courageous in his blindness than the philosophers and gods. Only little by little will he become accustomed to the brightness, seeing first only shadows and the reflections of objects in the water, then gradually the objects themselves, then the stars and the moon, and finally, last of all, the sun. Plato argues that the prisoner will eventually gain sight, will come to see the truth. But blindness has its virtues, too.

$$\blacksquare$$

Jake wasn't with me when I ran into Danny at Tia's, thank God. It wouldn't have happened if I had seen him first, but I was already up at the bar before I noticed him sitting at the far end.

"Hey," he said.

"Hey."

There was a longish pause. Charlie Blue came out the swinging door from the kitchen, saw us, and hightailed it back in.

"How's it going?" I asked.

"Fine."

Hank was sitting there, but he downed the end of his beer and hurried out the door without making eye contact. I looked around for the bartender, but no one appeared. Danny and I both tried to stare straight ahead, but there was a mirror behind the bar, so that didn't help. Danny developed a sudden absorbing interest in the takeout menu tacked to the wall by his shoulder. I studied the cigarette machine.

"Is anyone tending bar?" I said after a couple of minutes.

"He went to get ice."

"Oh."

We waited.

"In Alaska?"

Danny half-smiled but didn't say anything. He was peeling the label off his beer. We waited some more. I looked at him in the mirror behind the bar until he looked up and saw me.

"You're the one who left me," I said.

"Not for your best friend."

I saw the bartender peek through the little window in the kitchen door and then duck away.

"If your friends aren't allowed to date anyone you've slept with," I said, "they're going to have mighty slim pickings in this town."

"Don't pretend it was like that."

We glared at each other in the mirror.

"I don't want to fight with you," I said.

"That'll be a nice change."

"Oh, Jesus!" I shouted. "You're the one who cheated on me!"

He turned and looked at me face to face. His eyes had the blue shadows under them that I had seen the very first time we met. He needed a haircut, and his shirt looked slept in.

"If you keep yelling like that," he said evenly, "we'll never get a drink. The whole staff is frozen in fear behind that door."

"Cowards!"

"Well, at least they're not fools," he said, smiling.

"Not like us," I said.

"No," he said. "Not like us."

He put two dollars on the bar next to his empty beer bottle and got up. "I guess I'll see you around," he said.

"Yeah," I answered. "See ya."

He left and the bartender suddenly appeared.

"Sorry I took so long," he said, looking guilty. "What can I get you?"

"I need about seven hundred shots of tequila," I said. "But I'll start with one, and we can go from there."

Charlie Blue stuck his head out the kitchen door. "Coast clear?" he asked.

"Unless you count me," I said.

"Now that wasn't so bad, was it? Best just to go ahead and get it over with."

"Easy for you to say—I saw you lurking behind that door like the sniveling coward you are."

He smiled. "I was giving you privacy," he said.

"Thanks a lot."

"It'll be easier the next time."

"Maybe," I said. "In any case, it's over with now."

Danny had gotten rid of Tawni but went on to a string of other women whose names no one could ever keep straight, apparently not even Danny. Once he messed up and one of them tried to strangle him in broad daylight on Thornapple Street, but he didn't die, and the general consensus was that it probably did him some good, or at least that he probably deserved it. But even though he and I were friendly enough when we saw each other, I never went to the café anymore, and when closing time rolled around at the Cave every night, he was always already gone.

If Danny and I were awkward around each other, Danny and Jake were grim. Whenever they were forced by circumstances to speak to each other, they were just on the sullen side of icily polite, and on a few occasions I had to make myself scarce at delicate moments. Whenever this happened in the Cave, Rafi would look sorrowful—even more than usual—and Vera would look exasperated. The inevitable girl with Danny would look perplexed. Jake and I would look askance at each other all the next day or two, wounded in ways that we couldn't say out loud.

Fortunately, just at that time, a rich man uptown (we heard he was a big wheel in the Methodist church), following in the time-honored traditions of his ilk, figured out that there was almost as much money to be made in catering to the sins of the sinful as in fleecing the lambs of the church. Not quite, but almost. And what better way to honor Jesus, when you thought about it, than to convert the wages of the sinful into gold for the glory of God? He pledged his profits to Jesus. And if by "profits" he meant whatever he didn't spend on fancy cars and fancy suits and fancy women, he was no worse than most and distinctly better than many. The long and the short of it was that he decided to open a bar down on Juniper Street. He named the bar "Hell."

He left the running of the bar in the hands of some very capable and attractive boys whom he had met in ways that always remained obscure, but who knew enough to stock the jukebox with Muddy Waters and the coolers with Natty BoHo.

Hell was an immediate success. Part of this was because the downtown crowd, who took their fun where they could find it, reveled—for a while at least—in saying to each other, "I'll see you in Hell" or "Are you going to Hell?" or making elaborate and extended jokes revolving around the central idea that people in Hell want ice water, but that doesn't mean they get it. By the time they were weary of telling each other to go to Hell, they were habituated to the place.

At first, Vera worried some that the existence of Hell so close to the Cave would hurt her business, but the people who lived downtown were a thirsty bunch, and their capacity to absorb the new influx of beer into the local neighborhood was truly awe inspiring. Vera's profits suffered not even the slightest dip, and she and Pete would even visit Hell together every once in a while and drink a beer or two that weren't stocked at the Cave.

Hell was the perfect place for Jake and me. We would slump together in the darkest corner, feeling like outcasts, reading coverless copies of Plato or Rimbaud, and talking only to each other. We wore our most ragged clothes and smoked incessantly and looked sad.

The fact that our friends would hail us joyously whenever they saw us and join us in our corner and play "That's All Right, Mama" on the jukebox did have an unfortunate tendency to mitigate the overall dramatic effect of our tragic pose, and once Charlie Blue made me suddenly laugh so hard that beer came out my nose. But mostly we were successful at looking infinitely more angst ridden than we actually were. Jake was much better at it than I was.

With Billy Joe's help, Charlie Blue had not only finally learned to play his bass but could even manage to look up and smile while he was doing it. He no longer blushed and stammered whenever he got on stage, and what he lost in sweet-little-boy charm he made up for in stage presence. He would cut up some and tell bad jokes and crack himself up. Down in the Cave, he figured out how to hold our attention through a whole set. And if you can command the attention of a bar full of falling-down drunks who've already heard you play three times that week alone (once before at the Cave, once on the porch of the bookstore, and once—very faintly—from inside the kitchen at Blossom's), then you can command the attention of just about anybody. He got together a band called the Low Lifes—made up of a boy who worked at the copy shop, a boy who put up posters on telephone poles for a living, and two other dishwashers—and they hit the road. Charlie drove his uncle's old white van, and they played a different town every night, clear across the country.

When they made it back home, Jake and I drove over to Raleigh to see them play in a club that didn't even pass the hat, but charged three dollars beforehand at the door. We showed up at 11 P.M., and there was a line of people waiting to get in. When the Low Lifes took the stage at 1 A.M., the crowd went nuts. People were dancing so hard that the very air seemed to throb in time to the beat, and if you put your drink down on the bar, you could see the surface of the liquid shimmy in time to Charlie's bass line—*bompa-bompa-bompa-boom, bompa-bompa-bompa-boom*.

Charlie himself looked beautiful in the spotlight—long and lean like he was carved, only with a smile that flashed out to the crowd, drawing them to him. Two different girls climbed up on the stage and threw their arms around him and had to be dragged away by the bouncers.

We had never seen anything like it.

I looked at Jake, kind of amazed. "Charlie Blue," I prophesied, "is going to be a star."

Jake said, "Don't be so sure," but he was amazed, too. Charlie Blue was magnetic. The shyness we had seen at first had changed into a sultry, brooding charisma that was irresistible.

Although I had no previous experience with fortunetelling, it turned out I was right. A week later, the Low Lifes signed a recording contract with Pterodactyl Records and got an advance check for more money than any of them had earned their entire lives.

In his dialogue with Meno, Socrates lays out his theory of recollections. He argues that we are born knowing everything and only have to remember it. This is because the soul is immortal. It has always existed in the realm of truth before it is reincarnated into our mortal bodies.

But how can we learn to remember all the things our soul knows? Socrates says the soul's memories are stirred up like dreams. Like dreams, however, they mostly vanish in the light of day. Like dreams, they are fleeting.

There are things that I remember about Jake. I remember the view of his profile silhouetted by passing scenery as we drove down pine-bordered roads. I remember the sharp, quick way he inhaled a cigarette when he lit it. I remember the curve of his shoulder, the combination of softness and hardness of his arm. I remember him sitting at the bar with a beer and a lit cigarette beside him doing the crossword puzzle in the newspaper in ink. I remember him playing me a record on the child's portable record player he had at his house, happy to have me hear something he thought was great.

I don't remember what the record was. I don't remember lots of things.

Partly this is because we drank so much. But partly this is because that is the way of memory. Things we adore—things we think we will never forget—become so much a part of us that we become unconscious of them, like we become unconscious of breathing. After unconsciousness, oblivion. Those things are lost to us. We don't have any choice in the matter. The things we would rather forget haunt us, and the things we want to keep forever are gone.

Jake and I knew that even then. We talked about it.

"We never know what will be a memory," I said.

"Remember this," he said to me. "Remember this now."

We were just at that moment crossing a long, low bridge with shallow water spread out like a mirror on either side of us. Farther south, it would have been called a bayou, but here it was just water with low-hanging trees and scrub coming right down to the shore and even into the marshy fringe of the lake. Jake was drinking a beer, and the can was still cold enough to sweat a little. His dark hair was rumpled and standing on end. The sky was a perfect clear turquoise. I slid farther down on the seat and put my bare feet up on the dashboard.

"Okay," I said to Jake, "I'll remember."

The show I made of wanting to be left alone had no effect on Orla—unless it was to egg her on in her periodic visits.

"I tried to call," she announced gaily, pushing through the front door as soon as I, bleary eyed from sleep and wrapped in a blanket, cracked it open, "but no one answered the phone. I couldn't imagine where you would be at this time of morning."

It was eight o'clock.

"I was asleep," I said.

She snorted out a little laugh. "Time to get up!"

I might have told her to go, but Jake was fascinated by her and almost relished her visits. I could hear him scrabbling around for pants in the bedroom. He emerged looking tousled and beautifully devilish.

"Well, hey!" he would greet her, all smiles and eagerness.

Orla would turn to Jake. "Well, hello there," she would say, and there would be a pause while she stared at him as if trying to place him and then giving up. "How are *you*?" she would ask, with extra emphasis on *you* to cover up for not being able to remember his name.

"I'm great!" Jake would say, looking evangelically bright eyed. "How are you?"

And then Orla would launch into her story, telling him all about the "female trouble" being experienced by the cousin of a woman in her church or about the beleaguering foot problems being suffered by a friend of a friend. Jake would time her, surreptitiously glancing at the clock on the radio, to see how long she would go without his saying a word. I would leave them to it and get dressed and make coffee and sometimes even breakfast before she so much as paused for breath. The stories were always medical and vaguely gruesome. Her all-time record was forty-one minutes without a stop—this was when Lem's sister's hairdresser had to have a cyst drained.

Quite often, she brought something to give us—worn-out clothes of Lem's that were several inches too short and too wide for Jake, or church tracts for me. Once she brought us some leftover beef stew she had made.

"Lem and I ate all the meat and vegetables out of this," she said, "but the broth is still good, and that's where all the vitamins are anyway."

As she finally made her way out the door, she whispered to me, "Is that the same young man as the last time I was here?" When I told her it was, she leaned her head back through the door to call out cheerfully to Jake, "I'll be praying for your redemption from your sins!"

"Yours, too," she said to me, patting my hand and smiling.

I closed the door, and Jake laughed until he couldn't breathe. He was still laughing about it later that afternoon when we made our sinful way down to Hell.

♒

We met Vaslav in Hell.

He was Russian, from Leningrad, a refugee by way of Rome, Tel Aviv, New York, and San Francisco—just arrived in town. He was beautiful in the same lean, hard way that defecting ballet dancers were. His fingers and teeth were stained with nicotine, and his ice blue eyes were lazy and half closed. It was early afternoon, and he was very drunk.

He had come south, he said, after reading Faulkner, Capote, and Flannery O'Connor. He wanted to know if we could introduce him to Tennessee Williams. We could not, for many reasons, not the least of which was that Tennessee Williams was dead.

"What do you mean, dead?" he asked.

"I mean no longer alive," I said. "There aren't too many ways you can be dead."

"Ah, I am not so sure about that. It seems to me that there are many, many ways to be dead," Vaslav said. "How long has he been dead?"

"I'm not sure," I said. "Awhile—maybe ten years."

"It is so strange," he said. "It was not written about—his death—in the Soviet Union. But I should have known."

"Why, especially?"

Vaslav did not answer directly. "I wonder what else I was never told," he mused. "Of what did he die?"

"Nostalgia, I expect," said Jake.

"What is this—*nostalgia*?" Vaslav asked, looking perplexed. "A disease?"

"Yes," Jake answered. "A terrible one. It's when your face turns backward on your head and you become blind to everything around you and your heart starts to bleed very slowly but with nothing to stop it. Lots of Southern writers get it."

"Why?"

"I don't know," Jake said. "Probably something in the water."

Vaslav raised his glass of beer and laughed. "Good news, my friends!" he said. "We will always be safe from it then!"

We all clinked glasses.

He told us he had a suitcase full of songs that he was planning to sell in Nashville next month. He asked if we had ever been to Graceland and wondered how long the drive was—could we make it in one night? Jake, who was still giddy and sociable from his morning with Orla, was intrigued by this. He was not one to pass up an all-night drive, after all.

"It's thirteen hours to Memphis," Jake said. "But you can do it in ten—you know, if you drive at night. Nashville is closer."

"And you have friends we could stay with?" Vaslav asked, leaning closer to Jake.

Jake's eyes seemed to be looking at something very far away.

"Let me buy you another drink," Vaslav said.

We saw Vaslav almost every day after that.

During his speech in Plato's *Symposium*, Phaedrus tells us that Cupid was the child of Chaos. This makes sense. Other legends have Cupid as the child of Aphrodite, the goddess of beauty. But whoever his parent was, no one, god or human, could control him. Even mighty Zeus himself was powerless to resist Cupid's arrow. And Cupid was a wild, mischievous youth who relished the torment his arrows brought to those stricken with love. The turmoil he caused everywhere was such that if he was not in fact the child of Chaos, it was clear they were nevertheless close relatives. No one was safe—not even, as it turned out, Cupid himself.

It seems there was a mortal girl, Psyche, the youngest daughter of a king. Her beauty was so great that men traveled from all over Greece just to gaze at her in awe. Not even a goddess, they said—not even Aphrodite herself—could rival the beautiful Psyche. Men began to neglect the temples of Aphrodite and worship this girl instead.

The ancient gods were not a magnanimous bunch, and it was not long before Aphrodite swore vengeance against the hapless Psyche. She planned to induce Psyche to fall in love with and marry a ravening beast, in punishment for her beauty. The goddess called Cupid to bring his arrows and let them do their work against the girl. But here was Aphrodite's mistake: she thought that Cupid, the most feared of all the gods, could control the power of his arrows. That was not so.

From the heights of Olympus, Cupid looked down to the earth to aim his arrow, and there his eyes were arrested by the lovely face of Psyche, beautiful like no beauty he had ever imagined. Seeing her, his hand faltered on his bow, and in that instant, he was scratched by the razor-sharp tip of his own weapon. There was no hope. There was no reprieve. From that moment, Cupid was powerless in his love for the maiden.

There were travails, of course, before Cupid and Psyche could be together. And there was much treachery by Aphrodite in the meantime. But nothing, in the end, could overcome the power of Cupid's arrow. Their fates were sealed by the merest scratch of it. Eventually Psyche was made into a goddess.

No one—not Psyche or Aphrodite or Cupid—had planned this. Love upsets the plans of even the gods. And no one knows where Cupid's arrow will strike—not even Cupid himself. No one controls love.

Vaslav seduced everyone. The girls who had formerly devoted themselves to sighing over the loss of Billy Joe now fought to buy Vaslav drinks in Tia's. He charmed Vera by good-naturedly beating Rafi at chess and good-naturedly losing to her at pool. The burst of professor patronage following Tom's death had gradually dwindled, but now the bookstore became popular again. Even though we didn't sell many books, the store was almost crowded in the afternoons while Vaslav sat on the couch, passionate and funny, arguing about Eastern European economic policy, holding Emma Goldman in his lap. At times, it felt a little like Tom was still alive. He taught us all how to say "The workers control the means of production" in Russian. He held Bertie in his arms and danced her around the store singing, and then handed her back to Rosalita with tears in his eyes.

We took Vaslav with us to Lost Pond.

"No," Vaslav said, surveying our cheap vodka bobbing in the water. "No, no, no, no, no. You cannot drink this trash. I have something better."

And he did, producing from his bag three tiny glasses and an unlabeled bottle of water-clear liquid—Russian firewater that smelled like a meadow and kicked like gasoline.

"My grandmother makes this," he laughed, "in her bathtub." He took a sip and smiled. "I think she pisses in it."

He said, "You must not drink from the bottle anymore. You

have been drinking like capitalist pigs. I will teach you to drink properly—like Russians."

Sitting on the dock in the moonlight, he drank from the tiny glass with infinite, savoring tenderness.

"Do you smell the flowers?" he asked, holding out a glass to Jake. "Hold it on your tongue. Don't swallow yet. Wait. Wait. Wait. Now."

¶¶

Jake and Vaslav and I were sitting at the back-corner table in Hell. Hank Williams was on the jukebox, and Vaslav was singing along, quietly though—two-beer singing: "Hear that lonesome whippoorwill . . ." Vaslav knew all the words—all the words to everything.

"How do you do it?" I asked him. "How do you know the lyrics to all these old American songs? Did you ever hear them when you were a kid?"

"No. I never heard these songs in those days. I learned them all here when I came to America."

"Are you glad to be here?" I asked. (In the background, Hank's voice was breaking: "I'm so lonesome I could cry.") "I mean," I said, "I never asked you how you liked coming here."

Vaslav looked hard at his beer bottle, slowly running one fingertip down the side of the bottle, leaving a clear trail through the condensation.

"All I want," he said at last, "is one more day. One day where I could just sit in a room, nothing more, and know that Leningrad is outside the window." He looked up, and his eyes met Jake's. "I just want to feel it one more time again—feel that I am home."

"I know that feeling," Jake said.

"Maybe someday you could go back?" I offered.

"When I was growing up a little boy in Leningrad," Vaslav said, still looking at Jake, "you will laugh when I tell you this, but I loved oranges so much!"

"Oranges?" I said.

"You know, an orange was a great luxury for me then, in those days. I got an orange only one time, maybe two times, in a whole year. It was a big deal then for me to get this orange." He smiled.

"And then?" Jake said.

"And then I ate it!" Vaslav laughed. "I ate it and I was so happy! I was so happy—for days afterwards I had this happy feeling, this satisfaction, you know, because of that orange. The feeling lasted for a long time—longer than you would even believe."

"And then?" Jake said again.

"And then," Vaslav said, looking serious, "the longing would return to me. Slowly, but more all the time—this desire, this hunger. And I would think about it—the next orange—and I would long for it. When would my desire ever be satisfied again?

"So I came to the United States, and the first place I came was Brooklyn. And what was there? Right there at the corner of my street? The fruit stand—every kind of fruit in the world! And all so beautiful! Beautiful like only paintings or pictures in magazines could be! The oranges—hundreds of them—every day!

"When I found this place—this fruit stand—then every day I would go there and buy oranges. The man there laughed at me, but nice, you know? Nice laughter because I loved the oranges so much. And every day, I was happy. Every day, I had so easily the thing that I loved."

"And then you got sick of them, and now you hate oranges?" I asked.

"No," Vaslav said, looking grave. "No. An orange is a lovely fruit, you know."

He sighed. "But then after a little while, I felt it start to come back—this feeling of longing. I felt it begin again, begin to grow in me. Only now, there was a difference. The longing is there, but now I don't know what I am longing for. Now, in America, it seems to me that I can have anything—anything I want is here, ready in the stores, looking beautiful like paintings. I could have ten oranges every day—twenty, thirty. And everything is like that. So the longing now—what do I desire? What will bring me the satisfaction of one piece of fruit?"

He shook his head and drew another clear line with his fingertip down the side of the bottle. His fingers were stained with nicotine.

"Now that I can always eat, I am always hungry. I don't know anymore what it is that I desire. What I wish," Vaslav continued, "is that I could have just one day in Leningrad—one day when I knew that Leningrad was outside the walls of my room and that complete happiness is possible."

"Yes," Jake said. "You want to go home."

Vaslav laughed. "It doesn't exist anymore," he said, and got up to put another quarter in the jukebox and buy another round of beers.

Hank's voice warbled out, "Hear that lonesome whippoorwill . . ."

Naturally we expected that Vaslav's suitcase full of songs would either never materialize or, if it did, we would wish it hadn't. It's not that we had never listened, God knows, to less than stellar musical performances by our friends. We had, after all, watched Charlie Blue basically learn to play that bass while he was standing right on the stage. Happy to do it. What are friends for, if not to groan inwardly and still love you?

But Vaslav was different. He had come to us fully formed, descended from the clouds, knowing things we didn't know, having seen with his eyes things we had only dreamed. And to find him human, after all, and fallible—well, it would be disheartening.

But Vaslav talked about the suitcase full of songs all the time. He would bring it up casually in conversation—try to convince us to make the drive to Nashville with him. He was planning to head out, he said, just as soon as he could talk Billy Joe into going with him. Billy Joe, he felt, with his previous experience in Tennessee, was crucial to the success of this enterprise, although he assured Jake and me that we were also vitally important to him and that he would not even think of going without us. This went on for months, so that we got used to it and became habituated to thinking of Vaslav's suitcase full of songs as something that would always be in the future.

It was at Charlie Blue's going-away party that Vaslav played his songs for us for the first time. The Low Lifes were headed to New York to record their first album. Vera and Pete had a party for them out at their little house in the woods. The boys had to catch the plane at 8 A.M., which was perfect timing because it meant they would probably still be good and drunk when they touched down in the big city. We felt that no one should approach such a momentous occasion sober.

During the course of the night, Billy Joe played some and Pancho played some and Pamela sang with him. The Low Lifes played some and made funny, bragging, scared-shitless speeches. That was to be expected. But when Vaslav asked to borrow a guitar around 4 A.M., we were surprised.

I was standing next to Vera when he started to play. Her jaw dropped, and she stared at him open mouthed for a full minute before she finally shut it. Vaslav was good.

"I didn't know it was going to be like this," Vera said to me. "Did you expect that it was going to be like this?"

"I'm not sure I expected anything," I answered. "What did you think it was going to be like?"

"Well, I thought it would be, you know . . ."

"Terrible?"

"Russian." She stared at Vaslav. "And terrible," she admitted.

The songs were riveting. They were aching blues songs, driving rockabilly, stomping R&B, even twangy country tearjerkers. Vaslav knew how to write a hook, that's for sure. And somehow he managed to capture all kinds of myths and hopes and disillusioned dreams about America. I guess it was the effect of a long Leningrad childhood spent yearning for things far away.

"I assumed he was just full of shit when he talked about his songs," Vera said.

"Me, too," I said.

"I guess we were wrong."

"Looks that way."

He played for almost an hour—song after song. By the time he was done, Blossom was sitting in the corner wiping her eyes with a paper napkin and Charlie Blue was looking abashed.

"You know what?" Jake said to Vaslav, looking a little starry eyed. "We should take those songs to Nashville."

The only person who didn't fall in love with Vaslav was Danny. It's not that he disliked Vaslav or was ever unfriendly to him. Danny was constitutionally incapable, after all, of being unfriendly to anyone. It was just that sometimes when Vaslav was talking or was captivating us with stories and tales, I would notice that Danny's eyes looked uneasy or appraising. Just a flicker of doubt would shadow Danny's face and then be gone. I watched Danny watch Vaslav. I don't think anyone else noticed, though, except maybe Vaslav himself, who was always extra friendly to Danny.

"How are you doing?" Danny asked me, sitting at the bar in Hell, looking a little longer into my eyes than he needed to.

"I'm fine," I said, perplexed. "How are you?"

"I'm fine," Danny said kind of vaguely, like he was thinking of something else entirely.

Jake started spending a lot more time alone with Vaslav. The two of them would go off together in Vaslav's car and not be seen for hours and hours. Vaslav was fascinated by the abandoned cotton mill in Magnolia, and they spent whole days picking their way through the tangled scrub and kudzu outside or the litter and debris inside, talking, talking, talking.

Jake didn't come into the bookstore in the mornings so much. Instead I held Bertie while Rosalita filled in figures in the account books and shook her head and looked worried. Bertie could sit up by then, and she sat in my lap, plump and curly haired and honey scented. She was heavy with the voluptuous carelessness of a baby who has learned that everyone loves her.

I loved her. "Oh, my baby," I would say to her, "how beautiful you are," marveling at her tiny perfection and taking an unaccountable pride in rocking her to sleep. "Oh, my baby."

And she would snuggle into me.

Pancho came around a lot and sometimes would gently take the sleeping baby out of my arms, not waking her, and hold her for a while, rocking softly back and forth on his feet. He was still trying to touch the spirit world and began more and more to have a haunted look about him. Sometimes he came into the bookstore and paced around looking at the books and gingerly touching some of them with only the very tips of his fingers. Even though we spoke to him, he didn't hear us because he was concentrating, like when he tuned a piano. Then he would go over to the Cave and let himself in with the hidden key and play fiery Rachmaninoff sonatas so loudly that you could hear them if you stood in front of the bookstore.

Pancho never said whether or not he ever eventually made contact. I myself think that maybe anything is possible.

Truth be known, more of us than just Pancho were haunted by the ghost of Tom. Rafi, for example, developed complex feelings toward the coffee maker in the Cave on account of Tom's having drunk so many cups of greasy coffee out of it while sitting at the bar with Rafi on long afternoons. The coffee maker, formerly only an object of derision, became for Rafi a shrine. At first, he wouldn't make coffee in it anymore, treating it as sacred and therefore untouchable. But after some reflection, Rafi came to the conclusion that Tom would not have wanted the kind of veneration that kept him separate from the human bustle and life of the bar. Tom would have wanted to be part of the action. So Rafi began to make coffee again in the peaceful quiet before opening time. He always poured the first cup for Tom and set it in a little cleared space on the shelf next to the cigarette rack where it wouldn't get knocked over.

Later someone noticed that anyone who touched the coffee-pot by accident during the course of the day would be certain to have good luck that night. Billy Joe bumped into it while helping himself to cigarettes and then found a ten-dollar bill on the sidewalk. Vera collided with Rafi and jostled the coffeepot in the process and then didn't lose a single game of pool all night long. One of the busboys from Tia's knocked into it getting himself a beer after closing time and then went home and found a girl he thought he had lost forever waiting for him on his back steps.

You had to touch the coffee maker completely by accident, though—it didn't work if you touched it on purpose, although there were some people who didn't believe that. Hank, for one, touched it on purpose every day for a week, but as far as we knew he had no luck.

SNOWFALL

PANCHO, IT SEEMED TO ME, lived only in the Cave. I rarely saw him anywhere else—or if I did, say at the bookstore or taking a drink at Tia's with Pamela, he was only a brief visitor, soon to return to his home. I was wrong, of course. Pancho, too, had a whole life of his own. In fact, it turned out that Pancho had a secret life none of us even suspected. Fortunately.

When Pancho was just a kid, his mother had woken up one morning to find that the face of Jesus (if Jesus did in fact closely resemble a California surfer boy, as was popularly believed) had emerged in the tangled glory of the kudzu vine that covered practically the whole south side of their tiny house at the edge of the farm town where Pancho grew up. The image was clear as day, if you squinted some, formed from the very leaves themselves. The photographer from the local newspaper was sent to take a picture of it, and before she knew it, Pancho's mother had a phenomenon on her hands. The faithful came from as far away as Kansas to witness the "Miracle of God's Creation,"

"Our Lord Among the Leaves," "Our King Among the Kudzu." Pancho's mother, who enjoyed a good miracle as much as the next person, nevertheless figured that God was probably most likely to help those who helped themselves. She started charging a buck to view the vines—two bucks if you wanted to take a picture. She also sold ice-cream sandwiches (seventy-five cents) out of the deep freeze on the back porch and paper cups of ice water (a dime). By the time a cold spell caused the vine to die back to just looking like a regular vine again, she had taken in almost seventeen thousand dollars.

It was a miracle.

She put the money in U.S. government securities and in a couple of well-run high-tech start-ups, so that by the time she passed away and left everything to her only child, she was a surprisingly wealthy woman. Pancho never told anyone about this and never touched the money, being shy and a little embarrassed about it, and the interest just kept rolling in—more every year. We had no idea.

Rosalita had never married Tom. Even though there was no doubt that Tom would have legally claimed Bertie as his own child, he wasn't alive to do it by the time she was born. Nevertheless, after several months of lawyers filing paperwork, the bookstore became Bertie's inheritance from her father, held in trust for her by Rosalita. While this was lovely and entirely fitting in a symbolic way, in a financial way it was a mixed blessing at best.

Every month, Rosalita did the books, and every month the numbers looked worse. Rosalita worried and visited Tom's loan officer at the bank, and then she really worried. Creditors were patient at first, but they had businesses and families themselves and their patience couldn't last forever. Rosalita didn't complain, but there started to be a frown line between her eyebrows and an anxious look in her eyes.

Pancho noticed and, although he didn't say anything right away to Rosalita, he asked me, late one night while Rafi was restocking the beer and Vera was making out the deposit slip, if everything was okay at the bookstore.

"Well," I told him, "I'm not sure, but I think Rosalita is up against the wall. I think she's going to lose the store. Last time she paid me, she borrowed the money from Vera to do it."

Pancho didn't answer, just nodded his head, frowning. He spent a long time that night trying to touch the spirit world, and although he never said so, I think that in some way it's possible he might have finally had the success he was looking for.

The next day, Pancho made a visit to his own bank, where they were surprised to see him. Then he came by the bookstore, and he and Rosalita went out back and stood together talking in the yard. Forty-five minutes later, Pancho was flat broke and the bookstore was saved. Pancho made Rosalita promise not to tell anyone, and I'm sure she did her best. But as far as I know, after that Pancho never again paid for a meal at any restaurant in town or for a drink at any bar, no matter how much he tried to.

Eventually, Socrates says, the freed prisoner blinded by the glare of the sun would begin to adjust to the brightness. At first, he would be able to see only the shadows of objects in this new world.

Shadows are tantalizing. In themselves, they are nothing—only the absence of light. To see them is to see what is not there.

And yet, on the other hand, shadows are also premonitions of what is real and solid. Their existence as absence is dependent on the reality of a presence.

That is our fear of shadows. They are harbingers—but of what? What lurks behind them? In this, shadows call up all the terrors of our fevered imaginations. The unknown is filled with both dreams and nightmares. Shadows herald their arrival.

Chained in the pit of the cave, the prisoner had an intimate knowledge of shadows, formed his world from them. The routine of those shadows passing ceaselessly to and fro in the firelight was a comfort to him. These new shadows, though, presage the arrival of a dimly glimpsed new world. These shadows are the future. But will it be a future made of monsters or of something better?

The freed prisoner's eyes slowly adjust to the light. After shadows, he begins to see images reflected in water.

Reflections are tricky things. They are upside down or backward. Space is topsy-turvy and difficult to navigate. If you try to touch a reflection in water, it shatters.

But in that topsy-turvy world, we do begin to see—a tree, a cloud, a man. The images quiver and vanish, they stand on their heads, but they are there. And we are there. We can see ourselves among the reflections, trembling and fragile (as we always are) and upside down (as we often are), but there nonetheless.

The quiet pools of water in the new world are the first mirrors the freed prisoner has ever seen. Plato talks about his seeing the reflections of other things, other men. But standing with his head bowed by the edge of the water, the freed prisoner also sees, for the first time, himself.

Vaslav and Jake talked incessantly now about their plan of attack on Nashville and how they would conquer the music world there with Vaslav's songs—songs that Jake was collaborating on now, helping Vaslav to write. If Vaslav wasn't there, Jake and I talked about him anyway. We talked about how he would get on in Nashville. It had been a long time since I had slept in Jake's bed or even been alone with him at all.

And so I was glad and a little surprised when Jake came, one wintry Sunday morning, to my little shotgun house all by himself, bringing a sweet potato pie from Blossom's and coffee in paper cups. We ate the first piece of pie in the kitchen sitting at the table and the second piece in bed after we made love. The temperature was dropping, and we wrapped blankets around us and wished we had more coffee.

After a while, we got dressed and sat again in the kitchen. The light coming through the windows was silvery, reflected from the clouds riding low in the sky. Jake seemed far away, lost in thought, and his face reminded me of how it had been when we killed the squirrel.

"You have to do something you don't want to do," I finally said to him.

He looked at me, although not quite in the eye. "I guess," he said. Then he took a breath and looked at me straight. "I guess I have to tell you that I'm going away alone with Vaslav—to Nashville. I guess I'm in love with him."

It was like all the air was kicked out of my lungs. Like I had hit the ground hard. Like I was still falling.

"What?"

"I love him. I love him more than I can even say."

"I don't understand," I said. "What about us? What about you and me?"

"I can't help what I feel. I didn't mean for this to happen."

"You liar!" I yelled at him. "You are a liar! You lied to me! You made me think you loved me!"

"I thought . . . I really thought I did. I thought I loved you. And I do, but in a different way than I thought."

"But we belong together—you and me." I was crying now. "We're too much alike to be apart."

"No, we're too much alike to be together," he said. "I belong with Vaslav."

I was furious now. "Don't you say his name! Don't you say that bastard's name to me!"

"This isn't his fault."

"Don't defend him! He knew you were mine and he took you from me!"

"I was never yours," Jake said. "I was never anybody's—not until I found Vaslav. He's like a missing piece of me."

I was crying so hard that I was almost choking. I had a sick feeling, a sinking coldness in my guts. All those hours they had spent together while I stupidly waited for them to come back. Now it dawned on me what they were doing. I had been an idiot all over again, ignoring the truth just like I had with Danny. I should have known Jake was betraying me. I should have known all along that he would.

"You were in my bed ten minutes ago!" I screamed. "You were making love to me! What the fuck are you doing?"

"I wanted to say goodbye to you."

"A pity fuck? It was a fucking pity fuck? Fuck you, you fucking bastard! I never even liked you in the first place! You were the one who came after me! Get away from me—get the fuck out of my house! Get out!" And I slapped him in the face as hard as I could slap.

He didn't even flinch—just stood there and took it. But his eyes filled with tears, and he had to blink hard to hold them back. "I never meant any of this to happen," he said.

"Fuck you!" I screamed. "Get out of my life!"

Jake left my house and drove off in the dusk. I stood in the yard and watched the taillights of Vaslav's borrowed car disappear down the road. A snowflake drifted lazily down past my eyes. I looked up at the low, cloudy sky and saw that it was starting to snow and that the world was utterly silent.

If you have grown up with snow, you are used to it. But if you have not had much experience with snow, you know how confusing and disorienting it can be. Rain is different. Rain comes down in a way that is predictable, understandable, comforting. It mostly comes down straight—from the top of the world to the bottom. Even a driving, stinging rain, borne along by the wind, still comes down at a straight angle. Once you get your bearings by it, you can plod along under your umbrella, keeping your face dry.

There is nothing straight about snow. It whirls and drifts and meanders all over the sky, different flakes going up and down and sideways all at once. The snowflakes dance all around you, cavorting on a thousand eddies of imperceptible wind. If you look straight up during a rainstorm, you get wet. If you look straight up during a snowstorm, you get dizzy.

It seemed to me there was nothing predictable at all in the world just then. I felt that no matter what, I was doomed to be dizzy forever.

Orpheus was the greatest of all the mortal musicians, second

Sleeping with Danny again was a shock to my system for a couple of reasons.

The first was the collapse of time. Everything was just the same as it had been before—the way he tasted, the way he moved, the way he held me. It was as if all the months between then and now had never happened. Except, of course, that they *had* happened. Jake had happened. Between the last time I was in Danny's arms and this time, I had lived a whole separate life with Jake.

The second shocking thing about making love to Danny was discovering that I felt guilty for betraying Jake, which was pretty ironic, given the situation. I wondered if Jake—in Nashville by now probably, somewhere warm out of the snow with Vaslav—felt guilty about betraying me. ("Lay your sleeping head, my love, Human on my faithless arms.")

"Thinking about him?" Danny asked me in the silence.

"Does it show very much?"

"You're not quite as tough as you pretend to be."

"I still miss him," I said. "I'm sorry."

"No need to be sorry. It's no crime to sleep with one person while you're thinking about someone else." He grinned. "At least for my own sake, I hope it isn't."

"Cad."

"I don't think you'd mind knowing how much I thought about you," he said, pulling me closer.

"Don't add idle flattery to your list of sins," I said. "It's long enough as it is."

"Maybe. But you have to admit I have my good points."

I laughed. "One or two."

"Not as many as Jake, though?" he asked.

only to the god Apollo himself in the beauty of his playing. And Orpheus loved the maiden Eurydice with all his heart. Eurydice returned his love, and on their wedding day, she danced in joy across a sunlit field on her way to meet her bridegroom. But a viper lay hidden in the tall grasses, and as Eurydice went past, the viper struck out and bit her on the heel and Eurydice sank down dead.

There are not words enough to tell the anguish and grief of Orpheus. His terrible lamentations rang through the fields and forests. He determined to go into the depths of the underworld—whence no mortal came back—to plead with the god of the dead to return Eurydice to him.

He found the entrance to hell in a cleft in a cave and began the descent into the sulfurous darkness. The fearsome three-headed guard dog, Cerberus, rushed at him, growling and baring his blood-drenched fangs, but Orpheus began to play on his harp such lovely and beguiling melodies that soon the ferocious dog lay down and allowed him to pass.

So it went. The wondrous music of Orpheus provided his passport through the noisome wastes where the Furies spent their hours torturing the spirits of the dead for their sins, until at last he found his way to the throne room of the god of the underworld. Hades sat next to his queen, Persephone, and at their feet was Eurydice. Orpheus made his request—that his beloved be allowed to return with him to the world of mortals. And then, in the frozen suffocating gloom of the underworld, Orpheus began to play. And as he played his harp, the heart of Hades softened and relented. Orpheus was allowed to lead Eurydice out of the underworld, back to the world above—but only on the condition that he not look back at her until they emerged into the sunlight and the air.

And so, without looking behind him, Orpheus began to

trace his steps back. He led Eurydice through the dank and fetid caverns, past the lamentable damned—Tantalus, Sisyphus, Ixion—past the suffering Danaïds, past the slavering Cerberus, until finally a light appeared ahead of him. Orpheus felt once more the breath of earth upon his cheek.

All this time, he had heard no sound at all from Eurydice, and he began to fear she was not behind him after all, that he had lost her somewhere along the way or that Hades had broken his promise. With the sunlight just before him, Orpheus turned to catch a reassuring glimpse of his beloved. There was Eurydice, her lovely face still shadowed in the gloom. But just as his eyes found her and his promise was broken, Eurydice was taken, snatched instantly back into the depths, and only the whisper of a haunting farewell was left in her wake. She was gone.

Orpheus and Eurydice did not walk together, side by side, out of the underworld. When you no longer walk together with your love, you run the risk of losing them. The Greeks knew that when you lose someone you love, you may feel that you would walk through hell itself if only you could get them back. But no matter what you do, they will be lost forever just the same.

The snow that started then lasted for four days and four nights, although it might just as well have been forty, from my point of view. The drifts around my house got deeper and deeper until my winding little driveway took on all the characteristics of a mountain pass in Nepal—the kind where you want to make certain you're securely roped to an especially sure-footed Sherpa. The kind where any novices on their own would surely plunge to their deaths. I decided to stay inside.

The phone line went out during the first couple of hours, but the electricity miraculously held up, and I had plenty of canned tomatoes to live on in an emergency, having gotten custody of them in the split from Danny.

For the first three days, I was quite content to sit around moaning over Jake and eating canned tomatoes on toast. But by the fourth day, I became insufferable even to myself. So I was surprised and rather relieved when, on the afternoon of the fourth day, someone knocked on my door.

It was Danny. His jeans were wet with snow up past his knees. His cheeks were raw red from the cold, and he didn' have on any gloves.

"Good Lord, sugar!" I said. "What are you doing out in t apocalypse like this?"

"It looks like hell has finally frozen over," he said. "If member right, that was your condition for forgiving me."

I laughed. "Well, that was one of them, anyway."

"Why don't you let me inside your door and we car about the other ones."

"What makes you think you can handle the other one

"I bet if we put our minds to it," he grinned, "we can c some arrangement about them."

I felt a little breathless, like I always had around him

"Come on, sugar," he said. "If there's a snowball's cl hell, today is the day."

I laughed and stepped back and let him in the door off his too-thin coat and stamped the snow off his leg

"Are you okay?" he asked, looking serious now.

"You heard?"

"I heard."

"I'm okay," I said. "I'm better now." Then I lean and kissed him on his cold lips.

"I can't help it. I can't help missing him."

He sighed. "The heart is an unruly devil, that's for sure," he said.

"Lord, ain't it the truth."

In the morning, the sun was out and the snow-reflected light was hard and glittering. We had a friendly breakfast of canned tomatoes out of the jar together in the kitchen. Then Danny said goodbye.

"No regrets?" he asked, standing in the door.

"No regrets," I said. "I'm glad we're friends again."

Missing Jake was a fundamentally different experience from missing Danny.

Missing Danny had been loud—made loud by the presence of Danny all around town. The consolation drinking had been loud, incorporating both wailing and gnashing of teeth. Running into Danny by accident had been loud because it inevitably triggered the consolation drinking bouts. Even my new empty house had been loud because it was filled so often with my rowdy, supportive friends and, of course, with Jake.

Missing Jake was almost entirely silent, though, because Jake, unlike Danny, was gone. There was no running into Jake anywhere or any tussling over territory or friends. There were no late-night phone calls filled with tears and recrimination. There were no impromptu fights or fits of unexpected rage brought on by chance proximity. He just vanished. It was more like losing Tom than losing Danny. For all intents and purposes, Jake had died.

I was Jake's widow, but no one knew it except me. So while this had the effect of keeping the breakup *Sturm und Drang* to a minimum, it did open up novel possibilities for other types of action. In secret, I began my "Pilgrimage of Jake." Freed from the risk of running into Jake himself while I was doing it, I allowed myself to indulge in a lonesome and morbid daily round of visitations to all of his shrines. I could play his favorite songs on the jukebox in Hell in complete safety, no one but me and the vanished Jake even knowing they were his favorites. Jake would have known what I was doing, of course. But Jake wasn't there. I could drive down our old back-road haunts secure that he would never pass me going the other way and pity me. I walked by his house in the weed patch every afternoon, although after surprising the new tenant while he was taking a bath, I did stop looking in the windows.

I didn't moan about him down in the Cave, a respite for which everyone was grateful. I just quietly and determinedly lived in a world made entirely out of his absence, like living in a house where there has been a terrible fire. I mentally set up a cot in what used to be the bedroom and a camp stool in what used to be the living room, but there weren't any walls and everything smelled like smoke.

My friends were relieved because it seemed to them that I was doing fine. Rafi didn't need to push beers on me; Vera didn't need to lecture. Pancho played sonatas of heartbreak at 2 A.M., but they were for himself, not me.

Danny, of course, knew better, and we didn't sleep together again. Instead he became very gentle and brotherly with me, stopping by the house sometimes to see if I needed anything— groceries bought or spiders killed or lids taken off new jars—or eating breakfast with me in Blossom's and not saying much, but not asking me to say much either.

"I bought last time," he said without looking up from the newspaper when the check came.

"Cheapskate," I said. But I was relieved that he wasn't trying to be too kind to me.

One cold night, we sat together on my sofa and watched the Low Lifes make their first television appearance, playing a song from their new album on the *Late Show*. Charlie Blue joked around with the host and sounded witty and looked like a rock star, which I guess, in fact, he was.

"I gotta run, sugar," Danny said when the credits were rolling at the end of the show. "I'm late."

"What can you be late for at midnight?"

"There's a red-headed librarian waiting for me at Tia's. At least, I hope she's still there."

"Still?"

"Well, I might have told her ten o'clock."

"Bad man. Aren't you worried someone else might be snatching her up by now?"

"But think of all the fun I'll have trying to snatch her back."

"Are you ever going to grow up and learn to behave yourself?"

"Do you really want me to?"

"Not in the least."

Danny went out into the night, and I went to bed because I was feeling sleepy. I was sleepy all the time now. Widows are notoriously somnolent.

Without Jake around, I had no heart to find Orla's visits amusing. My intention was just to ignore her knocking on my door. Given that she usually came while I was still sleeping, this seemed like a workable plan. But Orla was nothing if not determined to give me the benefit of her company, and after three days running of getting no answer first thing in the morning, she shifted her strategy and ambushed me while I was hanging clothes on the line in the tepid winter afternoon sunlight.

"Hello!" she called out, crashing through the withered remains of my azalea bushes.

"Oh, hello," I said, startled, dropping my bag of clothespins so they scattered into the frost-crusted mud.

Orla watched me while I picked them all up, waiting patiently to explain to me why she was there.

"How are you?" I asked her.

"I'm good," she said, and then paused, looking at me expectantly.

"How's Lem?" I said.

"He's good," she chirped, still waiting for me to come out with it. I had no idea what she wanted, only that the ball was in my court. I cast around in my brain, trying to dredge up the name of one of her many medically challenged acquaintances about whom I could possibly inquire, but none came to mind, and I felt that I should have paid more attention during her previous visits. If Jake had been there, he would have remembered one of them. But Jake wasn't there.

Orla must have read my mind.

"Where's your friend?" she asked, looking all around the bleak little backyard, as if Jake might be hiding under the trampled remains of the azaleas.

"He's not here," I said as casually as I could, hoping I wouldn't cry.

"Hmm," Orla said, pursing her lips. "And here I was thinking that you had finally managed to catch someone."

I thought about Jake saying, "Remember this now," and about how the water on both sides of the bridge was smooth and still like a mirror.

"You're not getting any younger, you know," Orla said.

I thought about how the sky had been clear turquoise and about how the sunlight came in the car window and fell in a straight line across his hand on the steering wheel.

"By the time I was your age, I was married and had two babies," Orla said.

I remembered that the air coming in the open windows had smelled of pine trees, but that if I leaned closer, I could also smell, through the beer and the cigarettes, the faint earthy brown smell that was Jake.

"Why don't you ever marry any of these fellows you go around with?" Orla asked me.

For just that moment, the memory of him was so vivid that I swear I could taste him on my tongue.

"I don't know, Orla," I said.

The most beautiful of all mortal men was Adonis. Even the goddesses vied for his attention. But it was Aphrodite, the goddess of beauty and love, who lost herself most completely in him. She had been present at his birth and had loved him from the first minutes of his life. As he grew into a man, radiant and brave, she risked the wrath of her husband, Hephaestus, and her lover, Ares, the god of war, to be with him. Alas for Adonis, Aphrodite also incurred the wrath of her rivals, Persephone, the queen of the dead, and Artemis, the huntress.

The legends tell us that Adonis was fond of hunting and Aphrodite would sometimes join him, abandoning her silken robes and her perfumed couch to dress as a huntress herself and follow him through the woods. At other times, she would glide above him, riding across the sky in her chariot pulled by swans. It was on one such day that Adonis met his death.

He was on his own, hunting in a dense tangle of trees and underbrush, when he cornered a wild boar, ferocious and maddened with fear. Adonis drew his bow and sent an arrow directly to the heart of the beast. But Artemis, jealous of the preference that Adonis gave to Aphrodite, caused the arrow to go astray. Instead of killing the boar, it only wounded it, enraging it. In its pain, the boar rushed forward, goring Adonis with its vicious tusks, tearing the flesh that had been so perfect, ripping away his life.

Aphrodite, from her chariot in the sky, heard the death cry of her beloved. She swooped immediately down to his side, taking the bleeding Adonis in her arms. But it was too late. Adonis was dead, and all Aphrodite could do now was weep for him.

The legends tell us that as Aphrodite held Adonis in her arms there in the darkened woods, his blood fell drop by drop on to the forest floor, and where each drop fell, there sprang up a new flower—the blood-red anemone called the "windflower." They are his memorial.

The ancient Greeks knew that loss is not always the end. Something new can be born from every ending. Flowers can come from blood.

PANDORA

WEEKS AFTER THE SNOWSTORM, its remains still lingered on the shadowy sides of hills. One night, after the first day during which I made none of my usual Jake pilgrimages, I dreamt that I was in the driver's seat of a beat-up old car. The windows were down and I had a clear-eyed view of a wide horizon all around me. The car was parked at the pinnacle of a steep, rocky mountain. Next to me, riding shotgun, was a little boy. He was wearing sneakers and blue jeans with a ripped knee. He was sitting the way little kids do whenever their legs are too short for a big chair—his feet stuck out straight in front of him, dangling off the edge of the seat. He had storm gray eyes.

The car started to roll backward, down a rutted dirt road on the side of the mountain, picking up speed as it went. I was twisted in the seat, looking out the back window and trying to steer the car as we whipped around switchbacks trailing a cloud of dust, the wind blowing through the open windows. It was very tense and difficult. My heart was beating hard.

I looked at the little boy next to me. "We're totally out of control," I said to him.

"I know," he said, and smiled at me. "Isn't it great?"

When I woke up from the dream, I knew I was pregnant. The test I got from the drugstore later that week only confirmed it.

Prometheus, who was the cleverest of the Titans, stole fire from the gods and gave it to mankind. This angered the gods, and in retribution for this theft, Prometheus was chained by Zeus to a lonesome rocky peak in the Caucasus Mountains, where every day a bloodthirsty eagle swooped down and savagely tore out his liver and ate it. Every night, Prometheus's liver regrew, so he could suffer again tomorrow.

Having taken his revenge on Prometheus, Zeus then turned his attention to the punishment of mankind. Up until that time, there had been no women on the earth. Zeus's revenge was to give men Pandora, the first woman, the loveliest of maidens, endowed by the gods with every gift of grace and beauty. But the clever Zeus also gave his creation one fault, one single pernicious flaw. He gave her curiosity.

Zeus sent the misbegotten Pandora to earth to be the wife of Epimetheus, Prometheus's foolish brother. He sent with her a tightly sealed box, which he warned her never to open. He did not tell her what was in the box.

Zeus knew even then that Pandora was destined to engender the misery of humanity through her own action. He also knew that her action was inevitable, arising from her very nature as it was made by the gods. It is in the inherent nature of women, the Greeks say, to be curious, to wonder *what if*?

The gods—the vindictive, scheming, punishing gods—had

not long to wait before Pandora—in the night while Epimetheus slept—opened the box. Out flew all the plagues of humanity—greed and envy and slander, sorrow, mischief of every kind. These plagues buzzed around Pandora's head like wasps and stinging flies and then flew off to spread themselves throughout the world, causing grief wherever they went. But finally, last of all, from the very bottom of the box, out fluttered hope on tiny delicate wings. The sorrows would be with humanity forever now, but we would also have the fragile, sometimes imperceptible, wing beat of hope.

The story of Pandora tells us, if we brush away all the misogyny, that it is only those people—the Greeks call them women—who dare to embrace every part of themselves, who dare the bad with the good, the forbidden as well as the approved, the sins along with the virtues, who give us the saving grace of hope and who open for us the wild and limitless possibilities of wonder. It is only those flawed and tragically reckless rule breakers who ever find the answers to the question, what if? Maybe even from misbegotten people, millions upon millions of flawed Pandoras, there can come some good. Each of us, children as we are of that first woman, sometimes dares to open a forbidden box, and we must ever after brave the perils and demons that our own natures have brought upon us. But we have also, at the same time, released our own saving grace.

I doubt very much that I am the only person who ever thought about Pandora when deciding to have a baby. What if? we ask ourselves with wonder and awe.

It is lovely to have a secret, and at first I didn't tell anyone I was going to have a baby—a little boy, I was sure, with gray eyes.

The little boy was my secret companion, invisible and silent but magical, riding along everywhere with me, part of me.

The snow had melted and left the black tree trunks naked against the gray sky. Even the crows were silent now, and the hawks sat forlornly on high branches with their shoulders hunched against the empty air. But the little boy inside me was a warm vivid flame, a red glow that throbbed with every heartbeat. I carried him around, sheltered from the sharp winter cold, and he laughed with joy and made me laugh with joy also. We were happy to see the faded winter grasses ripple along the ground in the waves of icy wind. We were happy to see the pointed face of a fox peek at us from the edge of the woods and then disappear again into the shadows. I dreamt of the little boy clapping his hands in delight.

The thing about a secret pregnancy, though, is that eventually you're going to have to tell. Even if you don't tell, people are going to know.

I had two problems. Maybe three.

The first problem was how to break the news. The second problem was whom to break the news to. The third problem, which was only maybe a problem, was what to do then.

Maybe the baby was Jake's. Maybe he was Danny's. They bookended the snowstorm, the two of them, merging together in my memory along with the snow and the silence and the warmth of strong arms that held me tight in the violet dusk.

Jake was long gone. I hadn't heard a word from him since he drove off under the gray sky a lifetime ago. Yes, Jake was gone.

But Danny was right across town, pouring drinks at the café, telling jokes and laughing in the warm, coffee-scented air. Danny—who surely loved me as much as he had ever loved anyone.

I went uptown.

Danny was drying glasses behind the bar. The light coming in the big front windows filtered through a scrim of steam so that it diffused in a pearly glow all through the café. It reflected off the chrome cappuccino machine into Danny's eyes and made them seem especially bright.

"Hey, sugar," he said to me, smiling. "Where ya been?"

"Nowhere," I said. "Around. You know. Home. Around. Nowhere. You know."

Danny laughed. "Well," he said, "I'm glad we got that cleared up."

I felt sweaty and sick, like I had guzzled a whole bottle of cheap tequila in two minutes flat. I didn't know if it was nerves or the side effects of growing a human inside me.

Danny looked hard at me. "Are you okay?"

"Sugar," I said, "I gotta tell you something that you're not going to like."

"Come on out back," he said, and I went behind the bar and followed him through the kitchen and out the back door into the alleyway. I sat on an empty milk crate and he sat near me, resting on his heels with his back against the brick wall.

He lit a cigarette and looked up at the sky. Then he looked at me, and his eyes smiled. "It can't be that bad," he said softly.

So I told him—told him I was going to have a baby and that it might be his baby, but that it might be Jake's.

We sat quiet for a while, listening to the sounds in the alleyway—the low swish of cars on Juniper Street, the delicate clink of dishes in the kitchen of the café, Pamela's voice, too indistinct to make out the words, one sharp bark from a hidden dog.

"Scoot over," Danny said, and I inched a little bit to the edge of the milk crate. He sat down next to me, balancing on the rickety plastic, and put his arm around me. "I'll marry you," he said, and there was only the very tiniest pause before he said, "if you want me to."

I put my head on his shoulder like I used to in the old days when we sat at the corner table in the Cave and I watched him play cards. I tried to imagine us together again—like the old days, only with a little baby now.

But I couldn't see Danny and me together—I couldn't bring the images of it to my mind—because all I could see was my little gray-eyed boy. I could see my little boy's face, watching me, trusting me. He was depending on me.

Farther down the alley, I heard a screen door bang and a woman's voice call out goodbye. Danny was waiting for me to answer—I could feel him waiting, holding his breath. But I knew then that this little boy wasn't Danny's baby or Jake's baby. I knew then that this little boy was my baby.

"Thank you," I said to Danny. "I appreciate that. But it turns out that what I need most is just for you to be my friend. Be *our* friend."

His relief was palpable.

⁙

The bookstore, with Vaslav long gone, was its usual empty self when Rafi showed up the next morning. I was sitting on the sofa sifting through a big pile of childbirth books that Tom had ordered for Rosalita so long ago. The sunshine was pouring in the rippled window glass, and the dust was dancing in the beams of light. Rafi sat down next to me. I could tell by the look on his face that he knew.

"Oh, God," he said, picking up a copy of *Green Babies* and looking alarmed. "It's going to be green?"

I laughed.

"Jake?" he asked, looking serious again.

I shrugged. "Maybe. Does it matter?"

"Probably not—not if it doesn't matter to you, I guess."

"It's not that I don't care," I said. "It's just that I think we'll be okay without him. We will."

"We?"

"The two of us." I smiled. "There's two of us now. And we're in it together, for better or worse."

He reached over and held my hand. "You don't have to do this if you don't want to," he said.

"I know. I know that. I want to, though."

"Are you sure?"

"For the first time ever, actually."

"I'm glad then," he said. "Do you need anything? Money or . . . anything?"

"Oh, Rafi," I said. "Right now, right at this minute, I have everything I need."

He stayed with me all afternoon.

As the freed prisoner slowly sees more and more in his new world, Socrates says that his gaze shifts upward to the sky. At first, it is still too painful for him to look directly at the sky in daytime, with the burning light of the sun piercing his eyes. But at nighttime, he can study the heavens—the moon and the stars.

That is the word Socrates uses—he will *study* them. In this endeavor, he will not be alone. Humans have looked to the night sky to study the stars and the moon for eons. The sun beats down on us, and we lower our eyes before it. But the moon— how many generations of our ancestors have lingered in the night in order to gaze up at its mysteries, enraptured?

The moon is another world, perched just beyond our

fingertips. We can see its mountain ranges and its quiet deserts. We can imagine that perhaps we could make lives there somehow, deep in its tranquil valleys.

The freed prisoner has learned now that there is a world beyond the confines of the cave. And having made the journey to one new world, he looks up into the night sky and sees yet another, floating serenely above him. Perhaps he imagines there must be a tunnel to it somewhere. After all, he has no particular reason to end his journey now.

***

It is generally better for me to depend on my vices rather than my virtues. My virtues tend to be largely theoretical—I imagine that I might have them if only I were put into the right situation at the right time under the right attendant circumstances, etc. With my vices, on the other hand, I am on sure ground. They are not theoretical at all.

This dependability is not only comforting but also useful. For example, if I want to quit smoking, I increase my chances of success if I quit in the dead of winter—preferably when the forecast calls for freezing rain. It is far too much trouble to go out into the wind and the cold and the wet just to buy cigarettes—or at least my own laziness makes such a venture less likely. I bank on my vice of laziness to be strong enough to overcome any possibility of action. By the time I've conquered my sloth (or the weather clears up), I've gotten through the worst part of withdrawal. I always tell people who want to quit smoking that they should wait until February. It has worked for me—I have quit smoking lots of times.

Besides being cold and wet, I also hate vomiting. And that proved useful, too, because no sooner did I get good and pregnant than the list of things the smell of which made me vomit increased dramatically. And cigarette smoke was right at the top. I threw out a brand-new pack, washed everything in the house that was at all washable, filled the car ashtray with baking soda, and never looked back.

The downside was that I couldn't bear to be in the Cave— not only the smell of smoke but also the smell of beer made me wretched. One attempted afternoon visit was all it took. From then on, Rafi and Vera and Pancho visited me at the bookstore instead, where I could sit quietly on the couch eating plain saltine crackers and sipping stomach-soothing ginger tea per Rosalita's experienced advice. Though welcome, their visits exhausted me so much that I would go to bed at 8 P.M. and sleep for fourteen hours at a stretch. I was quite suddenly leading an alarmingly virtuous life. If the road to hell is paved with good intentions, the road to heaven is apparently paved with vomit. This must be yet another reason why virtuous people always look so sad.

🙊

"You missed a good band last night," Rafi said, sitting next to me on the bookstore couch while I slowly ate my crackers and his nephew Jordan lay on the rug looking at the pictures in Hamilton's *Mythology*.

"I was asleep," I said. "Or maybe puking. Probably puking."

"You would have fit right in with the frat boys."

"And yet I miss it."

"I'm becoming quite concerned," he said.

"About the puking?"

"About the baby."

"The doctor says I'm puking only a normal amount."

"Let's leave the puking aside for a minute."

"I thought you were concerned about it."

"I'm concerned about the baby," he said. "Pancho says that babies can hear things before they're born—in utero."

"You're concerned that the baby will hear me puking? And develop some sort of prenatal guilt complex?"

"Puking takes up a lot of your thought, doesn't it?"

"Puking takes up a lot of my day."

"Did I ever tell you that you're very glamorous?" he asked.

"No."

"This is why."

"You can have glamour or you can have babies. You can't have both," I said.

"I think we've strayed from the topic here," he said.

"I didn't realize we had a topic."

"The topic we have is that Pancho read this article," he said.

"Yes."

"And the article said that babies can hear in utero."

"Yes."

"And you're not coming into the Cave anymore now."

"Because of the puking."

"Leave it," he said, shaking his finger at me. "There is an important issue here."

"Which is?"

"I'm worried—Pancho and I are both worried—that your baby is not being properly prenatally exposed to the right kind of music."

"Dive-bar music?"

"Exactly. Is your baby hearing the blues? Being exposed to Muddy Waters? Does your baby even know who Robert Johnson is? If all it ever hears is the stuff they play in supermarkets and doctors' offices, it will grow up to be a fan of adult contemporary or Christian rock."

"Good Lord," I gasped. "I hadn't thought about it!"

"The dangers are very real."

"I see now that I've been flirting with disaster," I smiled.

He sighed. "You have to admit that you do love to flirt. It's part of your glamour."

So on rainy days when he wasn't working, Billy Joe brought his guitar over to my house and played old Delta blues to my belly. On sunny days, Pancho came by and sang all the separate parts of Renaissance madrigals, one by one, carefully explaining to my navel how the pieces were supposed to fit together. He would put his hands on either side of my belly and whisper softly into it long explanations of the historical development of polyphony in Western culture. It was remarkable how much he knew.

Blossom was a loving and generous woman. She would no more have let a person go hungry than she would have kicked a dog. Some days when times were bad, more people left the back door of her restaurant with a free supper in a box than ate out front at the tables. Her children were getting grown now, and even though they still worked in the restaurant, the two oldest boys had wives and homes of their own. Blossom was anxiously waiting for the first grandchild. In the meantime, she lavished attention and homemade applesauce on Bertie. And now she joyously opened her arms and her kitchen to me.

"Oh, honey," she said. "Sit right here. I've got a little piece of catfish fixed so nice just for you. It'll strengthen you." Sometimes it was chicken. Sometimes it was beef stew.

"You're going to be a mama now yourself," she said one day, looking solemn. "I had better teach you how to make pie."

I laughed. "It will be a long time before this baby will be old enough to eat pie!"

Blossom looked wistfully at her second-youngest daughter, tall and lovely, taking orders at the next table. "Oh," she said slowly, "it will be no time at all."

And so every afternoon for a week, I sat at the big table in the middle of Blossom's kitchen while she taught me to make pastry and then different fillings. Under her watchful eye, I beat eggs and creamed butter and slowly melted chocolate. Blossom wore the demeanor of a high priestess presiding over a sacred ritual, and I paid close attention to everything she said. My gray-eyed little boy slept peacefully inside me.

"Don't you worry, baby," Blossom said to me, even though I had never said anything about how scared I was sometimes. "If you feed them and you love them, everything else will take care of itself."

♥♥♥

By the time I heard from Jake at last, the baby was getting big in my belly and I could feel him moving, like a rustling of butterflies deep inside me. It was just a postcard, postmarked from Nevada:

> *Hope you are OK—Nashville horrible corporate suit nightmare—Vaslav never saw Vegas, so we are here— Had a good run at the tables—enough to get us to Brazil—leave tonight—Vaslav thinks Rio is the place to be—letter soon—I think of you. xx, Jake*

I put the postcard gently between the pages of *The Dialogues of Plato*, volume two, at the part of *Symposium* where Aristophanes explains that we all have another half of ourselves out there somewhere, that we are always searching for the part of ourselves that we lost when Zeus split human beings in half as punishment for our ambition. I tucked the postcard between the pages and then closed the book and put it away on the bookshelf.

HALCYON

CEYX WAS THE SON OF LUCIFER, the light bearer, and Halcyon was the daughter of Aeolus, the king of the winds. Their marriage was one of passionate love and enduring tenderness, and their home on the sunlit Grecian coast was filled with bliss. When Ceyx decided he must journey over the wild and storm-tossed seas in order to consult a distant oracle, Halcyon was filled with foreboding, a premonition of death. She begged him not to go, but even though he loved her, he would not stay. She stood on the rocky coast, desolate, and watched his boat vanish beyond the horizon.

The next day, alone and far from any shore, Ceyx fell prey to the tempestuous seas. The violent waves battered his boat to pieces, and Ceyx himself was dragged to the bottom of the sea and drowned.

Alone in her empty home, Halcyon kept vigil for her husband, praying to Hera every day for his safety, not knowing he was already dead. Finally, after many days, Halcyon's prayers touched the tender heart of Hera, and she had pity on the faithful woman. That night, Hera sent the god Morpheus to visit Halcyon in her sleep. Stealing into her room on silent wings, Morpheus took on the appearance of the dead Ceyx and, thus arrayed, touched the sleeping Halcyon and entered her dreams.

"Poor wife," he whispered to her, "I am dead. There is no hope for me anymore."

At first light, Halcyon, her heart heavy with dread, made her way to the lonely beach and gazed out to the sea. Far in the distance, she spied an object floating shoreward on the incoming tide. She waited and watched, her doom stealing inexorably upon her, as the object came nearer. At last, it reached the shallows in front of her, and she saw, as she knew she would, the dead body of her husband. With a cry, she flung herself into the water. But in that instant, the goddess Hera, from the boundless pity in her heart, transformed Halcyon. Instead of a grief-stricken widow, she had become a magnificent seabird. Ceyx, too, was transformed, rising from the sea on spreading wings. Halcyon soared over the water together with her mate. According to the Greeks, the two birds are seen together always, skimming across the waves, never parted.

And every year, Halcyon and Ceyx build a nest of twigs and flotsam and grasses that they gather from the beach. They build this nest not on the rocky cliffs or the branches of the olive trees or the sand dunes, but on the waves themselves, floating tremulously in the very heart of the swells. Halcyon is charmed, the Greeks say. Every year while she broods on her nest, with Ceyx watching over her, the restless seas become for once calm and tranquil. These are the halcyon days—the days of serenity, when the winds are soft and the seas are tamed, when the faithful Halcyon floats on her twig nest and waits for her children to be born.

Jake had said he would write from Rio, and I waited to hear from him. In the meantime, we all listened to the radio, hoping to hear of Vaslav or to hear one of his songs and find out that they had had some success somewhere. We all felt that songs as beautiful and haunting as Vaslav's couldn't possibly stay hidden forever. But time went by and we heard nothing on the radio, and no one in town heard from Jake.

Finally Danny drove me down to the state facility in Delphia one Thursday afternoon, and we asked the attendant on duty if we could see Jake's mother. But the attendant said we had to be on an approved list to get in, and we weren't. He said he was sorry there was nothing he could do for us.

So Danny told him that really all we wanted was to get in touch with Jake, and did he know if Jake had sent his mother any letters, or did she send him any, and where did she send them to? The attendant flicked his eyes down to my belly, where it was starting to be unmistakable that a baby was on the way.

"There are no letters," he said, shaking his head. "She's not . . . There really couldn't be any letters."

"Nothing coming in?" Danny asked him.

He looked sad and said again, "I'm sorry I can't help you."

In the lilac evening, Rosalita and I, each holding one of Bertie's hands, tottered gently down to the old wooden boat dock at Lost Pond. Bertie squealed with joy and paddled her baby feet in the warm water at the edge of the dock while Rosalita held her carefully around her chubby baby tummy. I sat with my feet in the water, too, getting splashed a little bit on my own swollen tummy. I remembered swimming here with Rosalita and Tom when it was Rosalita who was going to have a baby, the baby who was happily splashing me now.

The moon began to rise and the fireflies came out.

"I wish Tom were here," I said.

"Oh, he is," Rosalita answered me.

I looked at her.

"I feel him all the time," she said simply, stroking Bertie's auburn curls. "He's with us everywhere."

She smiled serenely into the soft darkness. Bertie stopped splashing and climbed into her mother's lap. The fireflies came closer, and Bertie clapped her hands, laughing in delight.

Rafi and I drove out to the abandoned cotton mill. The air in the old spinning room was sultry and still. Broken window glass crunched under our feet. The gray-eyed boy shifted inside me and then was still.

"Do you ever wonder if things had been different . . . ?" I stopped.

"What things?"

"I don't know. Like suppose Danny and Jake hadn't stayed late to play pool that night? Or suppose I had never asked for your newspaper that first day, the day I came to town? Suppose I had never come to this town at all? It was only by chance."

"I would have still been here," Rafi said.

"But you and I wouldn't know each other."

"No. But you would have met some other Rafi in some other town. And Vera would have hired some other barfly who was at hand at the time. I'd be standing here with a pregnant Hank, probably."

"But maybe there is no other Rafi," I said. "Maybe this is all destiny. Maybe you and I were meant for each other."

"Meant by whom?"

"Fate?"

"Maybe fate is what we call the lives we make for ourselves when we're trying to make sense out of what we did," he said.

"Maybe I fucked up when I ever looked at anyone but you. I should have just jumped you the first minute I set eyes on you."

"Maybe I'm not the pushover you think I am."

"Probably not," I sighed. "But anyway, now we'll never know."

"Besides, if everything had ended up different, you and I might have ended up hating each other."

"Oh, no," I said. "Lots of things might have been different, but not that. I never could have done anything but love you."

"Do you wish, though . . . ?" He stopped.

"What?"

"Do you wish things had been different?"

I stroked my belly and felt the butterflies rustle inside me. "Not really, I guess."

"Do you regret it?" he asked.

"No. Do you?"

"Only sometimes."

He took my hand and side by side we picked our way carefully out through the debris into the tangled, sunlit weeds outside.

That summer, songs from the Low Lifes' first album were everywhere, on all the radio stations, floating out the windows of the cars passing by on Juniper Street, playing on the little loudspeaker in front of the record store where Charlie Blue's picture smiled out from promotional materials and posters plastered all over the front windows. Vera got a tape from Charlie in the mail and played it in the Cave in the early evening before the night's band showed up. We saw the Low Lifes twice more on TV before they left for their world tour.

💢

I didn't grow a garden that summer—the gray-eyed baby, I felt, was enough for me. In July, I ate, at long last, the last jar of tomatoes. I ate them sitting at my little kitchen table during an afternoon thunderstorm. The rain hitting the tin roof of my shotgun shack sounded deafening at first, but as the storm spent itself, gradually the rain sounded only like rain.

"There, now," I said to the baby after I had eaten the last tomato. "From now on, I will grow just you."

💢

High summer came again, and wildflowers crowded together by the roadsides and in abandoned lots all over town. In the nicer neighborhoods, the yards had only grass; the flowers were strictly contained in carefully edged beds or in planters and porch pots. On the main square in town, the grand old magnolia trees opened their blossoms and the air all around was heady and lemon scented from them. But in the parts of town nearer to the river, black-eyed Susans and Queen Anne's lace and tiny, no-name pink and white daisies sprang up everywhere, even from the cracks in the cement sidewalks and between the steps of people's front porches.

Rafi and Jordan were out early one morning when they ran across Pancho holding a bunch of wild pasture roses. Rafi said he didn't think too much about it at the time, and it wasn't until he saw Pamela that afternoon with a pasture rose in her hair that he put two and two together. After that, Pamela came down to the Cave to play cards sometimes after she got off work, but more often Pancho went uptown at closing time and then walked her home in the warm night air.

ᵗ.ᵗ

"I don't suppose you ever hear from Jake at all, do you?" Vera asked me.

She had found a wooden rocking chair at the thrift shop and bought it and brought it to me. I was sitting in it on the porch and she was sitting on the steps, leaning back on her elbows.

"Not a word," I said.

"Do you suppose we ought to be worried that something has happened to him? Something bad? It seems like somebody would have heard something from him by now."

"Well, you know Jake. Just because he doesn't say anything, just because he doesn't write, it doesn't mean he isn't thinking about us."

"Do you miss him still?"

"Of course. Don't you?"

"Yes," she said. "But it's not the same for me as it is for you, is it?"

"I miss him," I said. "I miss him all the time. But at the same time, it's funny how I keep forgetting stuff."

"Like what?"

"I don't know. Little stuff. I can remember the color of his eyes and things like that, but I can't remember anymore—really remember exactly—what he tasted like."

I blushed. Vera laughed.

"Beer, I bet," she said.

I laughed, too. A sudden picture flashed across my mind and I saw the way his hand rested on the steering wheel.

"No wonder I can't remember," I said. "How long has it been since I tasted a beer?"

"I don't imagine you'll ever come down to the Cave much anymore now," Vera said.

"I'll come sometimes. But not much, I guess. It's probably not good for babies to spend too much time around Hank, after all."

"Not just babies—that could be hazardous to anyone's health."

"You'd better hope no one turns you in to OSHA for wantonly exposing your employees to him."

"Oh, he doesn't come around too much anymore. Word is that he and Stinky spend most of their time in the lounge at the Ramada Inn out by the airport."

"That sounds festive."

Vera rolled her eyes and shook her head.

"Do you suppose he'll ever come back?" she said.

"Stinky? Not if we're lucky."

"I mean Jake."

"Oh, I don't know. I imagine we'll see him again someday, maybe. Probably years from now," I said.

"You'll have a lot of explaining to do."

"I'll worry about that when the time comes. After all, who knows what things will be like by then?"

"I guess you're right," Vera said. "Life sure does have a way of changing."

"Anyway," I said, "he left us. He couldn't have thought everything here would stop and that we'd all stay the same as we were the day he drove away."

"But that is exactly what everyone always thinks, isn't it?"

"Maybe. They shouldn't, though. They should know better."

"Well," Vera said, "the things people should know better about—they make a long, long list."

In *Symposium*, Diotima asks Socrates, "What is the purpose of love?" and when he doesn't know, she answers that the purpose of love is to "give birth in beauty." This is cryptic even to Socrates, so Diotima explains.

Reproduction, she says, is as close as we humans can get to immortality. Because things to which we give birth—whether they are babies or poems or philosophical ideas—live on after us, partaking in a kind of immortality, it is in reproduction that we come closest to being like the gods. Through our offspring, and the offspring of our offspring, it is possible in a way for us to live forever. It is possible for us to be divine.

We are all pregnant, Diotima says—all of us, whether it is with babies or with ideas. And when the time is right, we all need to give birth to the things that are growing inside us. In order to be immortal, in order to be like the gods, we must release our children into the world.

But the purpose of love, Diotima says, is not just to give birth, but to give birth in beauty. We will give birth to our children only when we are surrounded by the good in spirit. We will bring our beloved children into the world only when the time is right, so they will be greeted by kindness and grace.

Pancho's generosity meant that we could order books again at the bookstore—not just textbooks for classes, but books to fill up the vacant places on the shelves, too. Rosalita and I worked together in the afternoon, flipping through the catalogs that publishers sent us, some still with Tom's name on the address labels.

"There are so many," I said to Rosalita. "How do we know which ones to get?"

"*No lo sé*," she said, turning the pages and looking quizzical.

"How did Tom decide?"

"He just knew," Rosalita said. "He had been to college, you know. Maybe he learned there."

We looked at each other across the pile of catalogs between us. I could tell we were both thinking the same thing.

"We should go to college," Rosalita said finally.

"You and me?"

"We could go together."

"How?"

"We will ask Rafi," Rosalita said. "He went to college. He will know what to do."

Rafi went with us the next day to the Extension School office at Waterville State and helped us look through the list of courses offered for the fall semester. Classes were scheduled to start right after Labor Day, and my baby was due right before then.

"How will I manage?" I asked them.

"We will help each other," Rosalita said.

"Everyone will help," Rafi said.

So Rosalita and I signed up for a class called "Great Books" that met once a week in the evening after the bookstore's closing time. Rafi helped us fill out the enrollment forms. The class cost four hundred dollars. I took the money that Uncle Joe had given me when I left home and handed it over. I had been saving it all this time. Rosalita looked solemn while she was filling out the forms, but when we got back to the bookstore afterward, she kept breaking into bright laughter at the thought of being a college student. Every time she laughed, Bertie would laugh, too.

"Tom is so happy," Rosalita said.

In the dog days of summer, even the bookstore stopped being cool. The dust sifting gently down onto the floorboards had a faint baked smell to it, as if we were making bread. Tom's coat was still hanging on the back of the door, but the smell of him had long since faded away, replaced by the slight stinging scent of pine resin in the heat.

The managers at Tia's ran the air conditioner out front where the tables were, but the kitchen was a sweltering steam bath. Two of the dishwashers even temporarily gave up smoking because, in a straw-that-broke-the-camel's-back kind of way, getting that close to lit matches was more than they could stand.

An argument broke out at the café uptown over the direction of the ceiling fans. Some of the staff argued that setting them to blow upward would pull the warm air to the ceiling and cool off the room. Others thought that was hogwash—and said so in terms considerably more direct than they were accustomed to using in cooler weather—and argued instead that they would rather have just the breeze. Everybody was looking a little peevish and sweaty around the eyeballs when Danny went down to the SaveMart and came back with a large supply of bags of discount frozen peas that the staff started wearing wrapped in dishcloths draped around the backs of their necks. This helped considerably.

Blossom managed to stay cool and sweet smelling all day, and when we asked her the secret, she told us that it was to think cool thoughts and to talk slower. I followed her advice as best I could but found that it worked most effectively if I practiced thinking cool thoughts while lying in a hammock under the shade trees in the backyard with a package of peas under me.

That's what I was doing the last time I ever spoke to Orla. I was just thinking about closing my eyes for an afternoon nap when her snapping-turtle face thrust itself around the corner of the house. She was moving much more quickly than Blossom would have recommended and started talking even before she was all the way into the yard. She had three worn-out, itchy-looking sweaters hanging over her arm, and I knew she had been cleaning out her closets and that I was once again the intended recipient of her charity, whether I liked it or not.

"I suppose you've been wondering why I haven't been by to see you in so long," she said. While I tried to gather up my heat-addled and scattered thoughts, she forged ahead into a preamble about rectal fissures. I swung the hammock back and tipped myself out of it and stood.

Orla gasped.

For one moment, there was a shocked silence with only the buzzing throb of the katydids to emphasize the sudden stillness. Orla gaped at me with her mouth open, and the sweaters fell to the ground. I put my hands protectively over my belly, and we stared across the distance at each other. I watched her face as she started to pinch it up, reminding me suddenly, vividly of Stinky.

"Are you pregnant?" she asked.

"Yes," I said, feeling the butterflies fluttering under my hands.

"Are you married?"

"No," I said. The butterflies were stronger now, like sparrows stretching their wings toward the sun. The gray-eyed little boy inside me was laughing in delight.

I tried not to think about Stinky much. But now, as Orla began to lecture me on my sins and mistakes, I couldn't get him out of my head. This would have no doubt surprised Orla, since Stinky was a vile drunk and Orla was a staunch and formidable pillar of her church. But there it was. Anyway, Orla was not pausing long enough for me to get a word in edgewise, so I couldn't have told her about this amazing mental conjunction even if I had wanted to.

"Let's kneel together," Orla was saying. "Kneel and beg God for forgiveness for your sins. Beg Him to stay His mighty vengeance against your iniquity, that it might not be visited on this child. Kneel and beg!"

Her words drifted slowly through the haze of heat, and it took me a minute to get the gist of what she was saying.

"But," I said, "isn't it . . . isn't it better to die standing than to live on your knees?"

Orla was momentarily perplexed by this, as if it seemed somehow familiar to her but she couldn't place it. She shifted tactics. "You don't even seem to care that this child you're bringing into the world will be a bastard. That's what everyone will say behind its back. A bastard."

I would like to report that I responded to this with an eloquent rebuttal, a moving defense of everything I held dear, an unassailable argument in favor of my life and my choices.

But that is not what happened.

"Orla," I said. "Fuck you."

She abandoned the sweaters lying on the ground, and later that afternoon I threw them in the trash.

THE ALLEGORY
OF THE CAVE

AT MIDNIGHT ON A CLEAR and moonless Saturday night, I went into labor. I was sound asleep, and in my dreams, a gray-eyed little boy was laughing. And then I was awake and I could feel, sure and certain, that this baby was ready to be born. I called Vera down at the Cave, and she left Rafi to take care of things there and went to wake up Blossom, and then the two of them came to get me. I sat out on the porch steps with my little suitcase next to me and waited for them in the cool night air. The stars were very bright.

While I waited in the dark, I imagined the scene at the Cave. The band was probably playing its first set, and the bar would be crowded with people who didn't know me at all, and Rafi would be working fast serving them beers. Pete and Pancho were most likely shooting pool together in the back room. I imagined them watching Vera leave and touching their beers together, and then Pancho would have a good run and sink the eight ball and Pete would go up front to pass the hat for the band. Danny was at the

211

café almost certainly flirting with a woman he had never met before and not knowing yet that this was a different night from other
ones. Two of the waitresses would be standing out in the alleyway
together sharing a cigarette and trying to hurry about it because
they had to get back inside. I imagined Rosalita asleep in Tom's
old iron bed with Bertie next to her, cradled gently in her arms.

¶¶¶

Blossom and Vera stayed with me at the hospital, taking turns holding my hand, until in the late afternoon my baby was finally born.

"I've never seen a newborn with eyes that color," the doctor
said while I held my slate-eyed little boy in my arms.

Blossom and Vera left after a while, both of them tired and
hungry. They were coming back later with catfish and biscuits
and pie. I sat in the hospital bed holding my sleeping child and
marveling at him. I didn't even hear the door to the room open,
but Danny appeared like magic beside me.

"Hey," he whispered.

"Hey," I said.

"Rafi came by and told me you were having the baby."

We sat side by side on the edge of the hospital bed. He was
looking at the baby and I was looking at him, thinking about
how many hundreds of times I had looked at his profile, how
well I knew his face, how his eyes looked tired now with the
translucent blue shadows I had seen from the very first and the
crow's-feet crinkling the corners that were new lately. I loved
him just at that moment as much as I had ever loved him.

He looked up and saw me looking at him. He smiled and
touched my face.

"The offer still stands," he whispered, "to marry you and be
a daddy to this baby."

I looked down at the tiny child in my arms—my baby.

"I know you would," I said. "And I love you. But you know this baby isn't yours. And this life that I'm going to have now isn't the life you ever wanted. I think that, for now, this life is just for this baby and me."

He smiled at me. "Well," he said, stroking my baby tenderly, "maybe so."

We stayed together like that for a long time. But he had a girl waiting for him downtown and he left after a while to meet her. I settled into bed with my baby in my arms and watched him sleep.

_W_

When Blossom and Vera came back, bringing my dinner, Rosalita and Bertie came with them. I sat in the bed eating the pie first because the future is always so uncertain, while Rosalita sat in a chair holding the baby and Bertie sat snuggled in Blossom's lap, gazing serenely at the newcomer.

"She doesn't mind you holding another child," Blossom said to Rosalita.

"_Esta es tu hermano,_" Rosalita said to Bertie. "This is your brother."

Bertie was getting sleepy and her eyelids flickered gently.

"It will be nice for them to have each other," Blossom said. "I always think it's nice when there's lots of other children in the family."

Vera laughed. "It's true," she said. "You don't get in half as much trouble by yourself."

"Yes," Rosalita said, smiling. "It's always better to have a comrade."

The babies were both asleep.

I brought my baby home from the hospital the next day. In the immense quiet of the house with all the trees surrounding it, the baby was a bright spot of warm and noisy life, concentrating in one place, so it seemed to me, the whole warmth of the sun, every gurgle of the river, every whisper of the wind, the very shout of creation.

Rocking my sleepy baby in my arms, I saw every dawn—every indigo, gray, rose-pink, well-remembered dawn—but I saw them through our bedroom window rather than through the opening door of the Cave. Sunrise meant for me the beginning of the day, rather than the end of the night.

It was a long time since I had been down in the Cave. So a few days later, in the early afternoon, I wrapped the baby up and we went downtown. I parked on Thornapple Street and picked my way carefully down the alley and then down the steps to the Ballroom Entrance. There was no one playing pool in the back room and no one at the bar except for Rafi, drying clean ashtrays with a towel and listening to the radio.

"Ah," he said when he saw me. "At last!"

He held my baby in his arms and crooned to him, swaying back and forth, while I finished drying the ashtrays and then took the covers off the pool tables and brushed them down. My baby had fallen asleep. But eventually two college boys came down the front stairs and wanted beers, so I carefully took the sleeping baby into my arms, kissed Rafi goodbye, and went out the back. Rafi held the door open for me because I had no free hands.

As I walked down the alleyway toward my car, the sleeping baby seemed extra heavy—as sleeping babies do. My arms felt very full and I thought then that I had never before realized how empty my arms used to be.

What would happen, Socrates asks Glaucon, if the former prisoner were to return into the depths of the cave and resume his old seat among his former fellows? His eyes, accustomed now to the bright light of the sun, would take time to adjust to the gloom. For a long while, the prisoner would be blind. And his former friends, observing his blindness upon returning, would conclude that the upper world is a place where one loses one's sight. The cave dwellers would believe that their friend has lost his senses and become a fool.

Socrates points out that the denizens of each place, the one above ground and the one below, would each have similar views of the other world that is not their own. Each would view the other as a place of blindness, a place to be risked only at one's peril. In some ways, both would be right. In choosing to live in one world, the prisoner must forsake the other. There is no way to live in both worlds without being regarded all the time as a fool, without returning continuously to blindness. Few of us have the strength for that. Socrates tells us that we will have to choose.

I didn't know Charlie Blue was in town. He snuck in quietly and lay low out at Vera and Pete's cabin in the woods. I was surprised when I found him at the barbecue joint out on the highway, sitting at the back corner table with Pamela.

"Charlie Blue," I said to him while he took my baby into his arms, making kissy-face sounds at him, "when did you get back home?"

"Oh, Josie," he said. "I'm not really here. I've got a new house out in L.A. that I should be in right now, but I just came back for two days to see about a couple of things. Tell me where this baby came from. I've been gone longer than I thought."

I ordered a plate of barbecue. "I would have thought by now you'd know all about where babies come from," I said. "The rock-star life must be more sheltered that I thought."

He grinned and blushed and looked just the same as he used to.

"What are you doing back in town?" I asked. "Is there no decent barbecue in Hollywood?"

"Girl," he said, "don't even get me started. The only food I get anymore is green algae shit and I don't know what all—kale and chard and shit like that." He shuddered.

"You gotta pay your dues, baby," I said.

"I thought that meant starving and freezing and having my fingers bleed—stuff I could handle. No one told me about the chard."

"Lord, how you suffer!" I laughed.

"Not that it's really so bad out there, though," he said, cutting his eyes over at Pamela. "I mean, there are compensations. Palm trees and sunshine all the time are nothing to sneeze at. You know—swimming pools, movie stars."

Pamela laughed and said to me, "Charlie has snuck back into town to invite me out to Hollywood to sing on his new record."

"It's going to be a smash, Miss Pamela," he said. "You're passing up a golden opportunity."

"Passing it up?" I said. "You've got such a great voice! You should do it!"

"Oh, I thought about it," she said. "But you know, it would mean being away from home an awful long time. And just right now, I kind of want to stick around here."

"Swimming pools . . . ," Charlie said in his most enticing voice.

"I've already got the pond."

" . . . mooooovie stars."

He flashed her his best beguiling smile and she laughed.

"And leave behind my glamorous life here?"

"Pancho could come with you, you know," he said. "They have out-of-tune pianos in Hollywood, too."

"Oh, maybe he would come," she said. "Probably so. But he'd always be missing home. We would both always be missing home."

Charlie looked out the window, blinking into the dappled sunlight. "It's not like you could never come back," he said.

"You haven't," she said.

"What are you talking about? I'm here right now!"

"I thought you said you weren't really here. Besides, it's not the same anymore, is it?"

"Do you want it always to be the same?"

"Yes," Pamela smiled. "Yes, I guess I do."

He shook his head. "There's a whole big world out there that you're missing out on."

"I've got a whole world right here," she said. "I would hate to lose it."

"You might get rich and famous," he said. "Wouldn't that make you happy?"

She laughed. "But I'm already happy!"

"I'm telling you, out in L.A., you can get everything your heart desires."

"Except good barbecue," she said.

He eyed my plate. "You going to finish that?" he asked.

"I'll share," I said, and he started right in on the hush puppies.

"There are some things you have to sacrifice for art," he said, talking with his mouth full. "I just wish good barbecue wasn't one of them."

Blossom's middle daughter, Amity, agreed to babysit for Rosalita and me when we went to our class. We were already waiting together at Rosalita's house when Amity showed up, followed two minutes later by Rafi.

"If Amity doesn't mind, I just thought I'd hang around," he said, looking sheepish. "In case she needs help or an errand run or anything."

"We'll only be gone an hour," Rosalita was saying when Billy Joe came in the door with his guitar.

"I thought it seemed like this might be a good time to give the babies some music," he said, looking from me to Rosalita to Rafi to Amity uncertainly. "If that's all right with you."

"It's fine," Rosalita said, "but we'll only be gone—"

"Hey, everybody." It was Blossom standing at the door with a pie in each hand. "I just thought I'd drop these by and see how everything was going. What are all y'all doing here?"

"*Vamonos*," Rosalita said to me, "before anyone else comes. We'll be late."

"Don't worry," Rafi said. "We've got everything covered."

I kissed my baby goodbye, and Rosalita and I got into my car and drove up to the college. We found the building and the classroom and nervously picked out two seats next to each other close to the door.

My baby had been born at the end of August. At the end of September, Uncle Joe took the bus all the way to Waterville to come see us. Danny picked him up at the bus station and brought him to my house. He looked just the same, smiled just the same. Only a little more gray hair and a few more laugh lines. He was wearing his best clothes for the visit.

"Well," he said, taking the baby in his arms, "let's see this fine young man here. Look at those eyes!"

"He's strong," I said. "That's for sure."

"Well, of course he is," said Uncle Joe. "Of course your child is strong."

"I haven't heard a word from Mama since I wrote her," I said. "Did she say anything to you about the baby?"

He shifted in his seat and looked uneasy. "Oh, Josie," he said. "You know your mama. She gets busy with things at hand. I guess you heard your cousin Belle's getting married, and your mama is all up in that, of course, running the arrangements and I don't know what all."

"Of course," I said.

"She did ask me what the child's name is going to be. You didn't say in your letter."

"I wanted to surprise you with your namesake, Uncle Joe. I named him after you."

"Well, now," Uncle Joe smiled, looking pleased. "Isn't that fine? Yes, he sure is a strong little devil. You ought to be proud."

We went to Blossom's restaurant for dinner and Blossom made a fuss over him, bringing him extra coffee and putting ice cream on his pie.

"I'm sure glad to know you're watching out for my girl," he said to Blossom as we were leaving.

Blossom patted his hand. "Don't you worry," she said.

We went to the bookstore the next day.

"All these books," he said. "I never seen anything like it. You have to wonder what's in them all."

The day after that, I put him back on the bus to go home.

"You let me know if you ever need anything," he said. "If you ever need anything at all, you hear?"

I kissed him goodbye and watched until the bus drove away. When I went home, I found a worn ten-dollar bill on the kitchen table with a note that said, "For my namesake. Love, Uncle Joe."

Every week all semester, Amity came by to watch the babies, and never once was she alone. Rafi came by, or Vera, whichever one wasn't working. Billy Joe brought his guitar a lot. Or Pancho and Pamela spent the evening, each holding a baby while they sang. As often as not, Rosalita and I would come back to find Blossom cutting pie for everyone in the kitchen and Danny sitting in the rocking chair, gingerly holding a sleeping child.

Eventually it seemed silly to pay rent on my house by the river, and Little Joe and I moved in with Rosalita and Bertie and Emma Goldman. I brought all my empty canning jars with me and we decided that, come spring, we would plant a garden.

With the savings on rent, I could afford to take another class at the college the next semester. I signed up for Small Business Management and Accounting.

Rosalita's eyes got big when she saw it on the list of available courses.

"*Dios mío*," she said. "Do you suppose that it is possible that we could make this bookstore profitable?"

"It's worth a shot," I said. "Miracles can happen."

"*Dios mío,*" she said again.

I never saw Jake again. When Jake's mother died, Blossom saw the notice in the newspaper. But there was no funeral service, and none of her sons ever came around.

I imagined sometimes that Little Joe had Jake's look around his eyes or maybe in the line of his jaw. But there was no address I could mail a snapshot to; I had no pictures of Jake that I could use to compare. Jake, wherever he was, never knew.

Above ground, the freed prisoner is finally able to see the sun. The sun is to him the light of truth and reason. Seeing all so clearly, he develops a new view of the world based on reality rather than supposition, objects rather than reflections, truth rather than shadow. He becomes, Socrates says, a philosopher.

Socrates argues that it is the duty of the philosopher to lead us all from the darkness of the cave, with its false understandings built only on shadows and echoes, out into the sunshine, where we will finally see the truth. In the light of true knowledge and reason, humans will at last come into our own.

I am sure that all of this is correct. It is famously hard, after all, to argue with Socrates. Better people than I have tried and failed.

And yet I wonder.

The enlightened philosophers, contemplating truth in the sharp glare of the sun—do they ever close their eyes against it, just for a moment, and remember fondly the beautiful, flickering blue shadows on the wall? Do they ever perhaps imagine they still hear—in the distance—the faint musical echoes of their old world? Standing even now on the very pinnacle of wisdom, do they ever sometimes quietly mourn the loss of their smoky, dreamlike, dusky cave?

ACKNOWLEDGMENTS

Thanks to everyone at John F. Blair, especially Anna B. Sutton who has made this book much better with her insightful eye, her poetic ear, and her generous heart. I am profoundly grateful and lucky to have worked with her; Amy Fusselman, who has been through thick and thin with me for many years, for offering encouragement and support and without whom this book never would have come out of the box; Jane Hilberry for nurturing a vision of wild creative possibility for me and for everyone around her; Steven Hayward for taking time from his own writing to give feedback that was both incisive and kind; Sandi Wong at Colorado College for giving me the time and the resources to go in new directions and for her friendship; a whole raft of people who used to hang out in a bar I knew a long time ago and who often saw me at my worst, yet never turned away; Paul and Bob for the music and the books; and to Jonathan, Aiden, and Tris for everything.